FIRE ON THE MOUNTAIN

ALSO BY TERRY BISSON

Wyrldmaker
Talking Man

TERRY BISSON

FIRE ON THE MOUNTAIN

ARBOR HOUSE/William Morrow

NEW YORK

Copyright © 1988 by Terry Bisson

Library of Congress Cataloging in Publication Data

Bisson, Terry.
Fire on the mountain.

I. Title.
PS3552.I7736F57   1988   813'.54   88-894
ISBN 1-55710-014-4

Manufactured in the United States of America
Published in Canada by Fitzhenry & Whiteside, Ltd.

10 9 8 7 6 5 4 3 2 1

*For Kuwasi Balagoon
and the Black Liberation Army
past, present and future*

Most of the good things in this book are from
Cheikh Anta Diop, W.E.B. DuBois, Leonard Ehrlich,
R.A. Lafferty, Truman Nelson, Mark Twain and
Malcolm X.
The bad things are, without exception, the author's own.

"The present, due to its staggering complexities, is almost as conjectural as the past."
—*George Jackson*

"Dawn also has its terrors."
—*Victor Hugo*

"America is our country, more than it is the whites' . . . we have enriched it with our blood and tears."
—*David Walker*

"My love to all who love their neighbors."
—*John Brown*

In 1859 the abolitionist John Brown, fresh from a successful guerrilla war that kept Kansas from entering the Union as a slave state, attacked the federal arsenal at Harper's Ferry, Virginia, with a small force of armed men. Brown came to Virginia to fulfill a lifelong dream: to carry the war against slavery "into Africa" (as he put it) by putting a small army of runaway slaves and abolitionists onto the Blue Ridge, and heading south. Brown's idea was that such a force, even if militarily weak, would terrorize the slave owners, embolden the slaves, and hasten the polarization which was already splitting the nation apart. Others obviously agreed: he had raised funds to buy the most modern weaponry, and recruited the experienced Black slavery-fighter, Harriet Tubman, to be his second-in-command.

The raid was symbolically timed for Independence Day, July 4, 1859; but Tubman fell sick and key supplies were delayed. After a three-month delay, Brown and twenty-one men struck Harper's Ferry on October 16, without Tubman. Through a combination of military errors and bad luck, they were cut off in the town and defeated by U.S. Marines led by a West Point graduate named Robert E. Lee. Brown and five others were hanged for "treason" and entered legend as martyrs instead of liberators. Even at the gallows they were dignified and unrepentant; even in failure, their raid terrorized the South, electrified the nation, and precipitated the Civil War, which broke out less than a year later.

Fire on the Mountain is a story of what might have happened if John Brown's raid had succeeded.

FIRE ON THE MOUNTAIN

Yasmin Abraham Martin Odinga drove across the border at noon. The man and woman at the station looked at her Nova Africa plates and Sea Islands University sticker and waved her on through without even asking for papers. Yasmin figured she was probably the first stranger they had seen all morning. Laurel Gap was not a busy crossing, and most of the traffic, from the looks of the road and the trucks and the area, was church picnickers and relatives home for Sunday visits—all known to them. Mostly white folks on either side of the border through here. Mostly older. Even socialist mountains give up their young to the cities.

An hour later Yasmin was in the Valley, heading north, with the high, straight, timbered wall of the Blue Ridge to her right, clothed in its October reds and golds. She scanned the radio back and forth between country on A.M. and sacred on A.X., ignoring the talk shows, enjoying the high silvery singing. There was no danger of running across the Mars news, not on Sunday morning here in what Leon had often impatiently but always affectionately called "the Holy Land." She eased on up to 90, 100, 120, enjoying the smooth power of the big Egyptian car. She had a 200-klick run down the valley to Staunton and she couldn't shake the uncomfortable feeling that she was late.

She was looking forward to seeing her mother-in-law, Pearl.

She was and she wasn't looking forward to seeing her daughter, Harriet.

She had something to tell them both, but it wasn't for them she was late. It was for the old man. She patted the ancient black leather doctor's bag beside her on the seat. In it were her

1

great-grandfather's papers, which she was taking to Harper's Ferry to be read on the hundredth anniversary of John Brown's Attack, fifty years after they were written, according to the old doctor's very precise instructions. Except that it was October and she was three months late. She had been asked to stay an extra month in Africa to finish the Olduvai Project; a month had turned into three, and she had missed the Fourth of July Centennial. A fax had been sent to the museum director, but it wasn't the same. Now she was bringing the original, according to the old man's will, in the stiff old pill-smelling doctor's bag that had held them for the thirty-six years since he had died (the year she was born), hoping maybe that it would make it up to him.

It's hard to know how to please the dead.

Near Roanoke she was slowed, then stopped, by buffalo. There was no hurrying the great herds that paced the continent's grassy corridors, east to west; they always had the right-of-way across highways and even borders. These were heading south and west toward Cumberland Gap, where even the mountains would stand aside to let them pass.

There was more traffic on toward Staunton: dairy tankers deadheading home for the weekend, vans of early apple pickers from Quebec and Canada, Sunday go-to-meeting buses—even a few cars, mostly little inertial hummers. Things were changing since the Second Revolutionary War. She heard more singing and reached over to scan the radio up, but it was the Atlanta–Baltimore airship, the silver-and-orange *John Brown,* motoring grandly past in the lee of the mountain; it sounded so joyful that Yasmin raced it for a few klicks before falling back and letting it go, worrying about potholes. The roads in the U.S.S.A. were still unrebuilt, wide but rough, straight and shabby, like the long, low, worn-out mountains themselves. Appalachia, on either side of the border, was a well-worn part of the world.

I am Dr. Abraham. When you read this, in 1959, what I have to say will be illuminated by the light of history, or perhaps obscured by the mists of time. Decide for yourself. I write as an old man (it is 1909), but I experienced these events as a boy. I was ignorant and profoundly so, for I was not only a n'African and doubly a slave (for no child is free) but an unlettered twelve-year-old unaware even of how unaware I was: of how vast was the world that awaited my knowing. There was only beginning to stir within me that eagerness, my enemies would say greed, for knowledge that has since guided, my enemies would say misled, my exact half century of steps thereafter. Fifty years ago today, in 1859, I was barely beginning to hunger and I knew not what I hungered for, for hunger was the natural state of affairs in the Shenandoah. Whatever the bourgeois historians tell us, and they are still among us, some in Party garb; whatever lies they might polish and toss, the slave South was a poor land. P-O-O-R. Great-grandson, do you even know what poor means fifty years in the future, in your day of social- ism, electricity, nitrogen-fed catfish, world peace, and mules so smart they would talk, if mules had anything in particular to say to us humans? In 1859 kids in Virginia and Caroline (called Carolina before Independence) didn't grow up, half of them— of us I mean; of "colored," which is what we were beginning to call ourselves, forgetting that we were Africans at all. We thought Africa was where the old folks went when they died, and why not? That was what the old folks told us. The Shenan- doah Valley was poor even for the whites, for it had the slavery without the cotton. There were plenty of what people called "poor whites." Nobody ever said "poor colored"; that went without saying, like cold snow or wet rain. Ignorance was the unshakable standard. The average man or woman, black or white, was as unlettered as a fencepost and about as ashamed of the deficiency. I could, in fact, read (this was my sworn secret from all but Mama and Cricket, for she had "learned me" my letters in the hope that someone, somehow, someday might teach me to do what she couldn't—combine them into words. And she was right, the trick was done by a tinker from Lebanon who laid up in our livery stable in the winter of '57 while he healed his bone-sick horse. Arabs know two things, horses and letters, and he taught me enough of both to get by. I had to bite my tongue whenever my master (for I was as owned as the Arab's horse), Joachim Deihl, gave up on a medicine label in frustration. But a "colored" boy reading was not to be tolerated even by a relatively tolerant Pennsylvania German like Deihl. Yes, I fought with John Brown. Old Captain John Brown, and Tubman, too. In fact, I helped bury the Old Man, as I will tell. I could show you his grave, but we swore an oath, six of us, six thousand of us, so I won't. If General Tubman is the Mother of Our Country and Frederick Douglass the Father, our Dixie Bolívar, then bloody old Shenandoah Brown, the scourge of Kansas, the avenging angel of Osawatomie and the Swamp of the Swan, the terror of the Blue Ridge, is some kind of Godfather. Blood may be thicker than water, but politics is thicker than either, great-grandson, and I loved the old man. I count myself as much his kin as any of his actual sons, that brave abolitionist family band who were the boldest of all his soldiers, willing even at times to stand up to their Captain, a thing which I saw no other (except Kagi) ever do. No, I never rode into battle with Captain John Brown, for he was too old and I was too young; he was as old as I am now, and I was as young as your own child, if you have one. But I fetched him his pot-boiled chicory-cut coffee on many a frosty morning while he and Tubman consulted with Green and stern Kagi: then I watched him while he watched them ride off to war; then he would sit by the fire reading his Bible and his Mazzini while his coffee got cold, while I helped Doc Hunter make his rounds, but always keeping one eye on the Old Man as the Doc ordered.

Many a frosty morning. Fifty years ago.

The backs of my hands on this typewriter tell me that I'm sixty-two now, an old man myself: but I was fourteen on those frosty wartime mountain mornings, sixteen when he died, and twelve when it all started on the Fourth of July, 1859, and it wasn't frosty that morning . . .

☆ ☆ ☆

Staunton was getting to be a big town. The three-county Red Star of the South Dairy Co-op and the smaller poultry- and catfish-processing plants were gradually luring the last of the small farmers down from the hills, and even a few of their children home from the Northern cities. The square ponds and dairies, the hillside orchards and flatland wheat stations up and down the valley were prospering. Yasmin only came to Virginia once a year, and even though she knew it was backward of her, she resented the changes that came with peace, socialism, and reconstruction: the new buildings, the treeless surbs, the smooth metalled streets. Staunton wasn't her hometown, it was Leon's and she resented the changes because he had never lived to see them; because they marked with architectural precision how long it had been since his spectacular, world-famous death. Five trips. Twenty seasons. Three new growstone overpasses. He was, this early autumn afternoon, four new morning schools, a hundred houses, and one new stadium dead.

It was ungenerous, Yasmin knew. After decades of under-development and years of civil war, the U.S.A., now the U.S.S.A., deserved a little prosperity. Leon, especially, would have wanted it. Leon, who had always loved his countrymen, even from exile. Leon, who had always welcomed the new.

5

* * *

Pearl, Leon's old-fashioned mother, lived near the center of town in the neat, tiny "rep" house that had been built ninety-five years ago for her grandfather: part of the reparations for the n'Africans who had elected to stay north of the border, in the U.S.A., after the Independence War. Whether they had moved south to Nova Africa or not, all black people had been covered by the settlement. The little frame house was perfectly painted and trimmed. Pearl shared it with another widow, also in her sixties, "a white lady, deaf as a post but a church member," according to Pearl.

Pearl had been expecting her daughter-in-law since noon; she came to the screen door with flour on her hands and tears in her eyes. Yasmin always made her ring-mother cry, then usually cried herself, once a year like a short, welcome rainy season.

But this year was different, and even though Yasmin looked for them, her own tears wouldn't come.

Harriet was at the Center, Pearl said—working on Sunday, was that what socialism was all about, come on in? Not that Harriet would ever even consider going to church; she was like her Daddy that way, God Rest His Soul, sit down. This was the week for the Mars landing, and Pearl found it hard to listen to on the radio until they had their feet on the ground, if ground was what they called it there, even though she wished them well, and prayed for them every night. God didn't care what planet you were on; have some iced tea. Or even if you weren't on one at all. Sugar? So Pearl hoped Yasmin didn't mind if the radio was off.

Yasmin didn't mind. She sat at the kitchen table and sipped that unchanging-as-the-mountains sweet Virginia iced tea that she had never been able to bring herself to tell Pearl she couldn't stand, listening to Pearl talk while she rolled out pie dough for the social at the church. What would God and Jesus do without

6

their pies? Yasmin wondered. They would neither of them ever have to find out. War, slavery, revolution, civil war, socialist reconstruction, nothing slacked the flow of chess, apple, pecan, and banana cream pies from the Appalachians. Pearl gave Yasmin the bowl to lick as if to remind her that, even at thirty-six, her boy's girl was still a kid to her.

Yasmin loved the tiny little woman with her seamed glowing face, tiny mahogany hands ghosted with flour, white hair like a veil, tied up; loved her in that way women never get to love their own mothers because there is not enough unsaid, and too much said, between them.

Still. She decided not to tell Pearl her news. She would tell Harriet first. That was only fair.

The house felt stuffy and, as always, too filled with junk. Walking through the tiny rooms, Yasmin found the usual holograms of Douglass, Tubman, and Jesus oppressive; the familiar P.A.S.A. cosmonaut photo, with Leon mugging at the end of the row, had finally stopped tearing at her heart and now only tugged at it like a child pulling a sleeve.

She clicked on the vid, and, at the sight of stars, as quickly clicked it off.

She decided to get her gifts out of the car.

Back in the kitchen, she helped Pearl tidy up and explained that she was only staying for the night. She had to leave first thing in the morning to take her great-grandfather's papers to Harper's Ferry, as specified in his will. Yes, she would be back to watch the Mars landing. Promise. Meanwhile, this was for Pearl. And she gave her ring-mother a helping basket from Arusha, showing her how it would grow or shrink, shaping itself to fit whatever was put into it.

"Wait till Katie Dee sees this," Pearl said. "She's deaf as a post, but she loves baskets."

"I didn't forget her. I brought her a scarf," Yasmin said,

7

realizing even as she said it that it was scarves, not baskets, that her ring-mother loved. Why did she always get the little things backward? "But wait till you see what I brought Harriet." She patted the flat little box on the table, not even aware that she was listening for them until she heard the clatter of feet on the porch, shouted good-bys, and Harriet burst through the door. Twelve last summer, still all legs and hands and feet. Bearing in her face like an undimmed ancient treasure her daddy's God-damn big brown eyes.

☆ ☆ ☆

On the Fourth of July, 1859, I was with old Deihl, winding up the Boonesborough Pike north of the Potomac, carrying a load of cedar posts to a cattleman in trade for a horse that was said to be lamed, but healed, but testy. Deihl owned a livery stable and speculated in "bad" horses. It was just before dawn on the Fourth of July. It wasn't our Independence Day then, great-grandson, like it is now, it was only theirs; but even "colored" boys like firecrackers, and I was busy figuring where I could get a few later that day. Old Deihl was snoring on the wagon seat as we passed a line of men in single file walking south, toward Harper's Ferry. They were all wrapped in cloaks, unusual for even a cool July morning, under which I caught—for a twelve-year-old misses nothing—the gleam of guns. At first I thought they were slave catchers with which the Shenandoah was well supplied in those days, but several were Africans like myself; also, there was something strange about a crew so big. I counted thirty. In the back walked an old man in a slightly comical peaked hat with ear flaps, stranger still on a July morn; and beside him, in a long wool scarf, a n'African woman carrying a tow sack by the neck like a chicken, only swinging slow and heavy, as if it had gold inside. All of the men in file looked away nervously as they passed, except one, who smiled shyly and

8

saluted me with two fingers. It's that little sad salute that I remember, after these fifty years. Though he seemed like a man to me then, at twelve, he was probably only a boy himself, maybe seventeen. He was white; I figure he was one of those who died, maybe gentle Coppoc or wild young Will Leeman; and I think he knew in his heart, for I am convinced boys know these things better than men, that he was marching off to die, and marching anyway—for what did he salute in me that morning, a skinny n'African kid on a jolting wagon seat: a brotherly soul? I was and still am at sixty-two. Maybe he was saying good-by to all the things boys love: the things the rest of us take a whole lifetime saying good-by to. But he went resolutely on, as they all did. Old Kate, Deihl's fifty-dollar wagon mule (he'd bought her for five) plodded steadily on up the pike, laying a rich, plunderous mule fart every hundred steps. Deihl snored on, put to sleep by them, as always. I've often thought that if I could have figured out a way to bottle mule farts and sell them back in the hills to old men, I could have stayed out of medicine altogether (and made several doctors I could mention happy, as well as myself; but that's another story). The woman, of course, was Tubman, with her big Allen & Thurber's .41 revolver, the very one that's in the Independence Museum in Charleston today. The old man was Brown in his Kansas war hat, given to him by a chief of the Ottawas, I forget his name. The rifles were all Sharps, as the Virginia militia was to find out the hard way. For though they were outnumbered, Brown's men had better weapons than any of the enemy they were to face over the next few years. At least in the beginning . . .

How do you tell your ring-mother you're pregnant? Especially when her son's been dead five years. Especially when his name happens to be on the damn vid every day. Especially when you're not married again. And don't want to be. And she's a Jubilation Baptist. And . . .

Yasmin would worry about it later, on the way back south to Nova Africa, after Harper's Ferry.

After telling Harriet.

They sat up not very late, the three of them, and talked of very little. Pearl was so uncurious about Africa that Yasmin wondered if she suspected something had happened there. Harriet went on and on about school. She had come to spend the usual month in Virginia with her granny; she had ended up starting school when her mother had been delayed two extra months in Dar es Salaam.

Yasmin's fingers were hungry to braid her daughter's hair, but Harriet had cut it almost too short, in the Merican style. So instead, she gave her her present. Excitedly, Harriet unwrapped the box and opened it. An icy little silver fog came out. Inside the box, nestled in sky blue moss, was a pair of slippers, as soft and formless as tiny gray clouds, but with thick cream-colored soles.

Pearl oohed and aahed, but Harriet looked puzzled.

"They're called living shoes," Yasmin said. "They're like the basket, only they change color and everything, and they never wear out. It's a new thing. They'll fit perfectly after a few days."

"Like yours?"

"No, these are just regular shoes." Yasmin held up one foot, enclothed in a golden brown African hightop of soft leather that shimmered like oil on water. "Yours are special, honey. The living shoes are something new, just developed; you can't even buy them yet. The Olduvai team helped get this pair from Kili especially for you. To apologize for keeping me over."

Harriet thought this over. So are they from you or them? she wondered. She picked up one slipper; it was warm and cold at the same time, and felt creepy. They looked like house slippers.

Why couldn't her mother have brought her beautiful shoes, like her own?

"The only thing is, they're like earrings," Yasmin said, kneeling down to slip the shoe on her daughter's foot. "Once you put them on, you have to leave them on for a week."

"A week?"

After Harriet went to bed, Yasmin sat up, brooding. "Don't be discouraged," Pearl said. "The child has missed you. Plus, even though she doesn't say it, all this Mars business troubles her too. Be patient with her.

"Now come over here, child, and let me fix your hair."

Harriet got up early so that she could walk to school with her friends one last time. It felt funny to want and not want something at the same time. She wanted to get home to Nova Africa, but she would miss her friends here in the U.S. She waited with the girls on the street in front of the school, hoping the bell would ring, hoping it wouldn't. The new shoes looked like house slippers with thick soles.

"Harriet, did you hurt your foot?" Betty Ann asked.

"My mother brought me these from Africa," Harriet said. "They're living shoes, so I can't take them off for a week. They're like earrings."

"They look nice," Lila said, trying to be nice.

"They don't look like earrings to me," Elizabeth said.

"They gave my granny shoes like that in the hospital," said Betty Ann. "And then she died."

"Oh, wow," the girls all said. Harriet's mother pulled up to the curb in her long university car, too early. The girls were used to the little inertial hummers, and the university's Egyptian sedan was twenty feet long. Its great hydrogen engine rumbled impressively. Harriet didn't tell them they were driving it because her mother was afraid to fly.

* * *

Yasmin watched from the car while the girls traded hugs and whispers and promises-to-write and shell rings—all but Harriet and one other, white girls; all in the current (apparently worldwide) teenage uniform of madras and rows of earrings in the Indian fashion. No boys yet. If Yasmin remembered correctly, they lurked in the background at this age, in clumps, indistinguishable like trees.

The precious living shoes she had brought her daughter looked shapeless and drab next to the cheap, bright, folded-over hightops the Merican girls were wearing. Yasmin watched as Harriet tried to hide her feet. Well, what did they know about shoes out here in the boondocks?

"What's this?" Harriet said, opening the car door and eyeing the doctor's bag on the front seat.

"This is your great-great-grandfather," Yasmin said. "Let's put him in the back seat. He won't mind. He's only twelve, anyway."

It was good to hear the child laugh. On the way down the Valley, Yasmin suggested to Harriet that after dropping off her great-great-grandfather's papers at the museum in Harper's Ferry, maybe they should spend the night. "It'll give us some time to hang out together before we head back to Charleston, and work, and school. I can tell you all about Africa."

Harriet liked that idea. She reached back and opened the bag. It had a funny pill smell.

"I knew great-granddaddy fought with Brown," she said. "I didn't know there were any secrets."

"Brown and Tubman," Yasmin corrected. Why was it always just Brown? "And it was great-great. And he didn't actually fight with them. And I didn't say secret papers. The story is the same one you've heard all your life in bits and pieces. He just wanted the original to be in the museum. This is the actual

12

paper that he wrote fifty years ago, in 1909. It's like a little piece of himself he wanted buried there."

"Creepy." Harriet closed the bag.

"Oh, Harriet! Anyway, I couldn't take it on the Fourth, since the dig wasn't finished yet, and—what with one thing and another, I was held up in Dar . . ."

There it was. Yasmin smiled secretly, feeling the little fire in her belly. At this stage it came and went at its own pleasure, but when it came it was very nice. ". . . so we're going now," she finished. "You and I."

"There was a big celebration on the Fourth," Harriet said. "I watched it on vid."

"Aren't you going to ask me about Africa?" Yasmin said, searching for a way to begin to tell her the good news. How do you tell your daughter you're pregnant? Especially when her father's never been buried? Especially when . . .

"Why didn't you ask me?" Harriet said.

"Ask you what?"

"Ask me to go. I could have taken the papers to Harper's Ferry. Then they would have been there for the Fourth."

Yasmin was embarrassed. It had never occurred to her.

"I'm his relative too. I was here the whole time."

The *Martin Delaney* motored past, but Yasmin didn't race it this time. The high whine of the differential plasma motors sounded complaining, not joyful. She searched her belly, but the little fire was gone.

The airship looked like an ice cream sandwich, with the ice-blue superconductor honeycomb, trailing mist, sandwiched between the dark cargo hull below and the excursion decks above. While Harriet watched, the honeycomb blinked rapidly: the ship was making a course correction, and it existed and didn't almost simultaneously for a few seconds. Then all was steady again. Weighing slightly less than nothing, and with slightly more

13

than infinite mass, it sailed northward as imperturbed as a planet in its orbit.

Harriet waved two fingers enviously as the ship glided away. From up there the world was beautiful. There was nothing to see from the ground but catfish ponds and wheat fields and country towns, one after another, as interesting as fence posts.

She punched on the radio, double-clicking on the news, then double-clicking again on Mars. Until her mother gave her that look.

"It's not that I'm not interested, honey," Yasmin said. "We'll be back at your grandmother's to watch the landing. I don't want her watching it alone. I just don't want to exactly hear the play-by-play until then, you understand?"

"Sure."

Two hours later, they were in Charles Town. Yasmin turned east at the courthouse toward Harper's Ferry. The road ran straight between well-kept farms, some still private. The wheat was still waiting for the international combine teams, working their way north from Nova Africa; but a few local hydrogen-powered corn pickers were out, their unmuffled internal-combustion engines rattling and snorting. Yasmin saw a green-gabled house at least a hundred years old and started to point it out to Harriet, thinking it was the very one in the story in the doctor's bag in the backseat, Green Gables. But no, hadn't that one burned? Besides, Harriet was asleep.

The shoes did look plain. There was something you were supposed to do with living shoes, to train them, but Yasmin couldn't remember what it was. She sighed. Her reunion with her daughter was not off to a very good start. Oh well, things could only get better. Ahead, the Blue Ridge, blue only from the east, was red and gold. Neatly tucked under it at the gap was Harper's Ferry, where the Independence War began.

☆ ☆ ☆

By noon I had unloaded the fence posts while Deihl dickered and spat in Low German with the owner, and we started back with the new horse tied to the wagon; he was indeed a skittery character. His name was Caesar, which I spelled in my mind, "Sees Her," for I had not yet formed that acquaintance with the classics which was to enrich my later years, and will I hope yours as well, great grandson. The owner, a breakaway Amish, said he had bought the horse lamed from two Tidewater gentlemen passing through; it made a Southern horse nervous, he joked, to live so close to the Mason-Dixon line, which ran, he said, at the very bottom of the field in which we stood. He pointed out the fence row. Sees Her munched hay out of the wagon bed as we headed back South, and Deihl unwrapped the sausage biscuits Mama had sent with us. Deihl was stingy with words, but he shared a pull of cider from the jug he kept under the seat; he was no respecter of youth in the matter of drink, but who was in those days? I lay out in the back of the wagon with my head under the seat out of the sun and went to sleep. Deihl went to sleep driving, and unless I miss my guess Kate went to sleep pulling, which mules can do. I was dreaming of soldiers, perhaps influenced by the little band I'd seen before dawn; or perhaps my second wife was right when she said I had the second sight; or perhaps the Amish was right and Sees Her smelled abolition; certainly he was to live the rest of his life surrounded by the smell: the horse woke me up whickering nervously. I sat up and heard popping that I thought at first was Fourth of July firecrackers. We were on the Maryland side of the Potomac, near Sandy Hook. The railroad bridge to the west was burning, or at least smoking mightily. A train was stopped on the Virginia side, leaking steam, and men with rifles were swarming all over it. Every once in a while one of them let off a shot toward the sky. A soldier watching from the riverbank

15

rode into town with us. Deihl didn't waste words asking what had happened because he knew we'd be told with no prompting. The town had been attacked by an army of a hundred abolitionists, the soldier said. He'd been sent with a detachment from Charles Town to guard the railroad bridge, but too late. The mayor, who was pretty universally liked, was dead, and so was a free black man named Hayward, who worked for the railroad. The soldier thought it was a great irony that a free "nigger" had been shot, since the attackers were "abs." The papers were to make much of this also: but since almost half the population of the Ferry was n'African, and almost half of that free, or what passed for free in those days, I don't know how it could have been otherwise. George Washington's grandson and a score of other Virginians had been killed, the soldier said. He had a chaw the size of a goiter and spat into the wagon straw, and I kept expecting Deihl to straighten him out, but he didn't. Coming past the end of the railroad bridge, we saw that the tracks had been spiked and two of the bridge pilings knocked over by a blast. The railroad workers were standing around looking either puzzled or disgusted, and one of them joined us for a ride across the wagon bridge into the town. He'd been drinking freely. He spat into the hay too, and still Deihl said nothing. I remember watching him spit uncorrected and thinking: what's this world coming to? Sees Her was tossing his head and whickering, but Kate was steady. In the town the hotel and several other buildings were still smoldering. There was a wild, scary smoke smell: the smell all of us in Virginia were to come in the next few years to recognize as the smell of war. There was no fighting, but armed men were all over the streets looking fierce, bored, and uneasy at the same time. I felt my black face shining provocatively and would have not hidden it, but damped its blackness down if I could. The railroad men and the soldier both said "Kansas Brown" was behind the raid, as if this name had deep significance. White folks made much of Brown,

16

though I had never heard his name, nor had any of the slaves until that day, when he became more famous among us than Moses at one stroke, and not as "Kansas" or "Osawatomie" Brown but as Shenandoah Brown. The railroad man told how the hotel had been torched and in the confusion Brown and his men had retreated across the Shenandoah into the Loudon Heights, which is what we called the Blue Ridge there. They had fast-firing breech-loading Sharps rifles. Once in the laurel thickets, who would follow them? "Not the Virginny milisshy," the soldier said, laughing. "They're at the tavern a-soaking their wounds in gov'mint whiskey." I will attempt no more dialect. The railroad man seemed to take the soldier's words for an insult and sulked and spat, wordless from there on. The soldier's cut was not altogether true, anyway, I found out later: four of the "Virginias" had been killed in the fighting before falling back, all upon one another. I felt a deep, harmonious excitement stealing over me, though I did not at that time truly understand the events or what they meant. Who did, Merican or n'African?

Deihl was in a hurry to get back to Charles Town, but he was a man of steady habits and so we had to stop at the Shenandoah Tavern, as usual. I stayed with the wagon. I usually took the chance when Deihl was in the tavern to poke around Harper's Ferry, but this day I felt I should stay with the tack; I have noticed in my sixty some odd years that in times of civil unrest even the most timid acquire a sudden ability to steal. Sees Her was still prancy and whickery, smelling abolition or blood or smoke, or whatever it was that agitated him. The steep and usually sleepy streets of Harper's Ferry were filled, and everybody seemed confused. Stranded train passengers were wandering around with slaves dragging their luggage behind them. I got off the wagon once, just to stretch, and a man with a Carolina accent tried to hand me his carpetbag to carry; after that I stayed glued to the wagon seat. Those Deep South types

17

thought every black face belonged to them. Sitting alone in the wagon, I was the only African in sight that wasn't hauling some white person's luggage around and I felt several curious looks, as though I were to blame for all the smoke and ashes (I hadn't yet seen any blood); perhaps it was my imagination, perhaps not. At first I shrank; then I sat up straight, experiencing fully for the first time that mingled sense of pride and terror that makes war such a favorite of men.

I saw an Irish boy I knew and hailed him, but he ran; I saw another boy I hardly knew and didn't like, and he stopped; he was black like me. This was my second lesson about war. It trues up the lines. The boy stopped at the wagon and in a conspiratorial whisper told me that two hundred "abs" had tried to burn the town and had shot the mayor dead. He sounded simultaneously shocked, scared, and boastful. Four of the raiders were buried in a common grave down on the river, he said; he'd tried to go down and see the bodies, but the soldiers were "thicker than flies." They weren't really soldiers anyhow, just Virginias, he said, with leftover Hall's pattern muskets from the Mexican War. The "abs" all had Kansas buffalo guns that would blow a man in half. Deihl came out and we headed home for Charles Town, six miles across the Valley. As usual when he had been at the tavern, Deihl was more talkative, which meant that he said about four words a mile. But I learned from him that rumors were flying: the "niggers" had all run away; the "niggers" had all joined Brown; the "niggers" were coming down from the mountain as soon as dark fell, with spears as tall as church steeples. In fact, later that week a wagonload of spears was found abandoned. Brown, or some of his backers, had obviously figured the slaves wouldn't know how to use rifles. Aaron Stevens, a military man and one of Brown's commanders (after Kagi and Green), and I met again thirty years later, in Ireland, in '89, when I was chief surgeon at the Medical

Center in Dublin. Stevens was dying of cancer, for which there was then no cure. He yearned to talk of old times, as dying soldiers do. He told me, laughing, that it had taken the average black slave who joined them "a full thirty seconds" to become deadly with the Sharps. The fact was, hardly any slaves joined Brown at first anyway. Mostly we n'Africans were waiting to see, waiting to see. Even the few who had joined him in the excitement of the raid (he had passed out rifles, not spears) had stayed behind rather than follow across the river and up the mountain, perhaps mistaking his retreat for a defeat. Some pretended to have been kidnapped and told fantastic tales: which is probably the origin of the story that Lewis Washington, George Washington's grandson, had been shot by Brown while quoting Patrick Henry. I knew the man, for Deihl had sold him a team of mules, which he abused so scandalously that I had to go fetch them back. He was no Patrick Henry quoter. The fact was, I found out later, Washington was killed by a stray bullet from the militia, and Brown never intended to kill him at all, which was a sore point between Brown and his soldiers, who wanted no hostages. As to the story about the spears, maybe Deihl believed it, or maybe it was Kate: anyway, we got to Charles Town in record time, long before darkness fell.

☆ ☆ ☆

The Harper's Ferry Museum was filled with dead things. Rifles that hadn't been fired in a hundred years and would never be fired again; wool coats with bullet holes in them, one with blood splashed all over the collar. Swords, spears, pistols, knives. Harriet was sick of history. First a famous father, now a famous great-grandfather. Great-great. There was no room for real life. Her famous father crowded out the real father she loved remembering. Her mother spent her life digging up bones.

19

Scuffling along in her ploddy new shoes, she followed her mother through the dim, almost deserted museum, trying to keep her eyes from alighting on any of the exhibits, resisting their power with her own.

The Second International Mars Expedition was just making sub-Deimos orbital insertion as Yasmin entered the museum director's office, according to the vid on the wall behind his desk. Grissom stood up and punched it off, coming around the corner of his desk to meet his guest. Yasmin had heard that he was in the war, but she hadn't known he was missing a leg. She could see that standing up was his way of letting people know it, so they wouldn't be caught off guard. A one-legged man was a shock, almost as old-fashioned as the artifacts out in the museum.

He scanned down the vid—also considerately, she suspected: guessing, correctly, that it might be painful to her.

Still, she was glad to know that the boys and girls were safely through the Door, as Leon had called it: the Deimos Door. He was always very romantic about anything having to do with Mars.

"Scott Grissom."

"I'm Dr. Abraham's great-granddaughter, Yasmin. And this is his great-great . . ."

But somehow, Harriet was not behind her. She had gone off somewhere. Well, let her explore. Or sulk. Or whatever. Kids loved old guns.

Yasmin knew Grissom had fought in 1948, in the Second Revolutionary War, so she'd had him figured for a man about her own age. She was surprised to see he was twenty years older, in his late fifties at least. She was also a little surprised that he was white, since even after a hundred years, even after a war and a revolution and almost ten years of building socialism, most of the Mericans who admired Brown and Tubman were black, like her mother-in-law.

Yasmin handed Grissom the doctor's bag, and Grissom turned it over as if he were trying to find the spot where he could see through it. He looked at Yasmin and she nodded and he opened it. He grinned at the rich smell of old pills, and Yasmin decided she liked him. He took out the crinkly typed papers and hefted them, smacked them, turned them over, sniffed them like a scholar or a hound dog.

"So," he said, "the ancient family destiny fulfilled."

Yasmin nodded. "They're yours now. I'm leaving the bag with them. I think that's what he would have wanted."

"Thanks," Grissom said. "On behalf of the Revolutionary Park Service—and personally. I feel like I know the old man after reading the fax you sent. He was a particular old soul, wasn't he? He expected his papers to be opened and read right here, last Fourth of July, exactly one-hundred years after the raid, to the day . . ." He regretted saying this as soon as he saw her face cloud over.

"He expected me to be a great-grand*son,* too, you might have noticed, if you read them." It irritated Yasmin that this man, like her dead ancestor, like so many men in her life, didn't realize that she had other things to do than participate in their ceremonies. "As I explained in my letter, I was delayed in Africa and couldn't . . ."

"Oh, I didn't mean . . . I know you've been at Olduvai. After I got your letter I read the article in *Scientific African* about the dig. What did you call it? 'Million-year-old dirty dishes.' "

Yasmin rewarded him with a thin smile. "A woman's lot."

"All I meant was, better late than never." Again. One foot and he couldn't keep it out of his mouth. "Anyway, I do hope you both can stay a few days. I've arranged a room at the Shenandoah if you'll be the guest of the museum."

21

"Oh, I'm afraid not," Yasmin said. "I'm due in Staunton tomorrow, and Nova Africa Friday."

"But Mother, you said we were going to stay a night," Harriet protested from the doorway. "Please?"

What was this, forgiveness?

"This must be the old man's great-great you were telling me about," Grissom said. He saw a tall young woman with a broad moon face—like her father—in the doorway, keeping her back to the old Sharps and Hall's rifles and the coats with bullet holes in them. Like most teenagers, she seemed to regard museums as assaults on the very principles of youth.

Grissom got up and took her hand. "And how did you like Africa?"

"I didn't go. I've been in Virginia all summer with my grandmother."

"We really don't have the time to stay," Yasmin said. "I'm due in Staunton tomorrow, and Nova Africa Friday."

"You stay in hotels all the time," Harriet complained. "I never get to stay in a hotel. With a six-track I'll bet."

"In every room," Grissom said. "Oh, are those living shoes?"

"They're new," Yasmin said. She noticed they had changed a little. The left one was darker today and went farther up Harriet's ankle. "I mean, just developed."

"I know, I read about them. A new substance, grown only in zero-gravity tanks on Kilimanjaro. The first creation of a new life mode in space."

"Really?" Harriet said, almost smiling. "They feel okay."

"They get prettier, too," Yasmin said. She decided she liked Grissom after all. But when she'd been told the shoes were from Kilimanjaro, she'd thought people meant the mountain, not the orbital station.

"Please stay at least a night or two," Grissom said. "I was hoping to show you around the area. You're part of our history here, you know, through your great-grandfather. Plus, I have someone I want you to meet. Remember the letters that I wrote you about in Africa?"

Letters? Yasmin tried to remember: something about a doctor.

"What letters?" Harriet asked.

"Old, old letters," Grissom said. He fumbled through the junk on his desk and pulled out a pile of yellowed papers, handwritten, tied with pink ribbon. He handed them directly to Harriet. "A hundred years old. They're from the abolitionist doctor who taught your great-great-grandfather medicine."

☆ ☆ ☆

July 7, 1859
Miss Emily Pern
11 Commerce St.
New York

Dear Miss Pern:

Everyone here in Philadelphia is talking of the Events at Harper's Ferry. I don't mind telling you it has set the Cause back a hundred years. I suspect you and I will disagree on that, but so be it; we can discuss it when I am next in New York, which, God willing and exams be done, will be next month early. I don't think violence will do anything but enrage the Southerners, and I speak knowingly, being for better or worse, one of them. Not that I am enraged, just worried.

What if Brown's attack had failed? Such an under-taking, unfortunate as its effects are now, would have been Disastrous had the abolitionists fallen into the hands of Virginia. Imagine, abolitionists hanged for Treason! I fear it will happen yet; they are for now high in the Blue Ridge, but in the long run they are doomed.

No slaves joined them and none will. Violence will never free the slave, not only because he is so outnumbered, but because violence is foreign to his nature. I hasten to add: whatsoever my Reason tells me, my Heart is with those who oppose slavery, however I may abhor their methods. Let me tell you a story in strictest confidence. Amazingly, I had, it seems, foreknowledge of Brown's raid. In June my father had a stroke, which he survived, but in a weakened state. I was called home to Staunton for a week and returned north with my uncle, Reuben Hunter, the Attorney, of Baltimore, my father's younger brother. Uncle Reuben is forty, between my father and myself in age. Far from resenting the fact that Mint Springs was entailed to my father (and thus to me), he is quite solicitous of the Hunter family honor, and even goes beyond, affecting all the airs of a planter: and even presumes to instruct me in how a Virginia gentleman should act. Needless to say, I never discuss with him my sentiments toward abolition. In short, we're not close, but blood is thicker than water, and I agreed to ride with him from Winchester, where he had bought two horses, to Baltimore, and proceed by train from there back to school in Philadelphia. It was on this journey, some five miles north of Harper's Ferry, that we saw a young woman hanging wash outside a little dogtrot house on the mountainside on the Boonesborough Pike. Uncle Reuben pranced his new horse Caesar (which was quite skitterish) across the lawn to ask for water. We didn't need water, of course, we'd just forded Sassafrass Creek a half mile back, but Uncle Reuben, though married, loves to play the bachelor, at least when his wife's not around, and show off his traps and manners, sweeping his hat off his head like a Tidewater planter. I stayed

24

on the road since I find these mannerisms ignorant and degrading, not only to the women who must endure them, but to his family and to himself. Of course, since he is my uncle, and I not his, I cannot protest. I happened to hear a clatter from upstairs in the house and looked up and saw—I suppose it doesn't hurt to tell it now, and to a true abolitionist such as yourself—a negro in the window holding not just a rifle but what I recognized as a new pattern Sharps. Alarmed, I looked out for Uncle Reuben, who was getting a frosty welcome from the woman (whose accent was unexpectedly Northern). Not to be deterred, he was about to dismount, when the door slams and out of the house rushes an old colored mammy, a hanky on her head, her aprons flying, clucking like a hen, swinging a tow sack—Lawdy, Massa! she started yelling that he was trampling her—yarbs 'n' narstrums—and boldly grabbing Caesar's bit, she led the horse back out to the road while its rider looked back helplessly, longingly, and fetchingly, I suppose he imagined, toward the lady. I have known Uncle Reuben to whip slaves like an Irishman, but he was too much playing the gallant to even speak harshly to the old Mammy in front of her lady (plus, he could not trust his horse). By the time I looked back up at the window, the negro with the Sharps had gone. I was careful never to say a word of this to anyone, for I figured we'd stumbled across a Way Station (for fugitive slaves) and that was that, though a Way Station with armed Negroes seemed a sinister thing. Little did I know that what was being planned was a bloody raid in which the innocent would die. Did you know that the first to be murdered at Harper's Ferry was a free colored man, not a slave but a Citizen of the town? The whole country knows this Osawatomie

Brown from Kansas, where he gave abolition a dark name killing five men coldbloodedly in the Swamp of the Swan, with a sword. All the same, I'm glad to see a blow struck against slavery. To be fair I must admit that many here in abolitionist circles admire Brown, more than will announce or own it. Caesar turned even more skitterish and went lame later that day, and Uncle Reuben swore the old Mammy'd hexed him. We had to sell the horse for half his price and then buy another at twice, for Uncle Reuben's pride will not allow him to seat a plain mount. Some say Brown made the raid to steal guns for Kansas, where he plans a free-state empire. Others say he's arming the slaves to massacre whites.

As for me, I think violence only makes the Negro's situation worse, as well as being foreign to his Nature.

I appreciated your frank letter and hope to see you again very soon. I sincerely admire your determination to study medicine, but I hardly think Boston will be more friendly to the idea of a female doctor than New York, or even the hidebound South itself. Your friend and future Colleague,

> In the Cause,
> Thos. Hunter, Esq, M.D. *(ad imminen)*
> Philadelphia

☆ ☆ ☆

"Ow. Mother! Grandma already did that."

"Hush. Sit still, honey. Let your mama fix your hair."

"No, later, please. I want to watch vid."

Yasmin gave up, got a shawl, and went outside, onto the little terrace that opened from the room. It was almost dark. Yasmin didn't usually like to be outside at night under the stars, but here it was okay: the bulk of the mountain covered half the sky like a comforter pulled up under the eyes, and the clouds took care of the rest. The Shenandoah Inn was almost empty; the hotelkeeper had explained that it was late for tourists and that travelers usually stayed in the more modern Bolivar Hotel up the bluff, toward Charles Town, which had a shuttle to the airship hold. It was cool here under the mountain and Yasmin liked that: now, again, she could feel the little fire inside her, too small to light or heat anything but itself; not quite a person, but certainly a life. She sat with the old letters on her lap, not reading them but listening to the river, invisible behind the trees. The yellow poplar leaves shook as if applauding a show she didn't have tickets to. The Shenandoah River sounded cold and rocky and indifferent, not like the muddy, friendly little Caroline rivers that just sort of sat with you. Behind her she could hear bits and pieces of the news on vid as Harriet scanned through, then double-clicked on the Mars voyage. Why shouldn't she? The ship was named after her father.

Yasmin's husband, Leon, had been killed in space five years before, on the return from the first Mars flyby. In Africa this summer, as part of the antiquities team for the Olduvai extension of the Great Rift Expressway, it had seemed especially ironic to Yasmin that she was relocating the graveyards of people who had tied their children's braids a hundred thousand years before; she was repairing the pots they buried their loved ones with, while the father of her child, the comrade of her days, the lover of her nights, hadn't even left her with a body to bury. The accident, a welding line break, had happened during an EVA, in deep space, in slow motion: the whole world listening across a hundred sixty million miles while Leon, spinning irretrievably away from the ship, assessed the damage for his comrades, outlined the fix (he was Chief Engineer), and said farewell. Farewell. Harriet was eight. Leon was so far away that

27

he had already been dead for 14.5 minutes when he said good-bye to her and Yasmin.

It had broken the child's heart, but broken hearts children get over with. It had left Yasmin alone, and afraid of the night sky. She couldn't stand to look at the stars. Where was Leon in all that cold splendor? She hated the shroudlike Milky Way, or in Africa, the Southern Cross; she hated the million brilliant stars looking like candles in a graveyard endlessly deep. Of course, she knew it was morbid. For five years she had never told anyone, not even Harriet, why she stayed inside at night: with Leon gone there was no one to tell. Until last summer. And she had told Ntoli not because they were lovers (she had had lovers) but because he was old enough, in his spirit, to understand. He had that formal southern African fashion of answering a touch with a story, a story with a touch. In the traditional fishing villages east of the Cape, he said, when a man was lost at sea his belongings were buried so that the Earth would not forget him.

His own father was buried so.

Harriet scanned the vid down farther; she could tell by the way her mother sat holding her shoulders that she could hear. She clicked through the menu. Land reclamation in Europe was going well. In Timor they were farming the sea. The *Lion* was in sub-Deimos orbit, where the crew was programming the great ramwings, preparing to descend. Click, click. "Like the cellular memory of a limb that has been lost to evolution," the vid explained, "the pseudo-wings align and guide the ship in an imitation of flight appropriate for the rarified air of the red planet."

Harriet was still young enough, at thirteen, to understand remembering something she'd never had. Her father had once told her that gliding was easier the younger you were, because almost everybody remembers how to fly from their baby

28

dreams. As they grow up they forget. Even after he became a space engineer, he loved gliding.

Harriet was going to start flying this year whether her mother liked it or not. The collective would back her up.

She punched off the vid, and went to the door and looked out onto the terrace. Her mother was asleep with the letters on her lap. Even though she had gotten along fine for the summer, even though she was almost thirteen, which was almost fifteen, which was almost sixteen, Harriet was glad to have her mother back. Even a cranky mother who was afraid of the sky. Harriet covered her with a blanket and took the letters inside to read. She reached down to take her shoes off, then remembered that she couldn't. But she could: they flexed to help her. She stepped back into them and they put themselves back on. That was neat.

But if they were going to get pretty, she wished they would get on with it.

Yasmin was dreaming of Leon again. It was the same dream she'd had twice since coming back from Africa. Leon had been a gliding instructor in college, but he had never asked her to go up, understanding that she hated flying (which was why she'd taken the car from Nova Africa, after grinding her teeth for four hours on the triplesonic from Dar). But in the dream he didn't understand anymore. He was like a stranger. He reached for her and she pulled away. He didn't look right. He was wearing the space suit he wore in the stupid holo at his mother's house, the one he was wearing right now, 14.5 minutes ago. Up there. I can't go with you, Yasmin said. He got smaller when she said it.

I can't go with you.

He got smaller when she said it.

She woke up in a cold sweat. No wonder: the clouds were gone, and the million stars were glaring down at her over the mountain. Trembling, she gathered up her blanket and went inside. It wasn't true that the dead wanted you to be happy; they resented being dead alone. Harriet was asleep on the couch. The letters were at her feet, arranged in chronological order. One shoe had dropped off, and when Yasmin slipped it onto her daughter's foot, the shoe helped out. They would be great for babies. Babies wouldn't care how they looked.

She laid down with her little fire. She decided to tell Harriet that she was pregnant tomorrow, then tell Pearl the next day, when they were back in Staunton on the way home to Nova Africa. Watching the Mars landing while Pearl wept. Yasmin wasn't looking forward to any of it.

☆ ☆ ☆

It seemed I had a horse. Deihl wanted Sees Her gentled, so he didn't mind me riding him night or day. That night I went to see Cricket out at Green Gables, the plantation two miles out of town where Mama had lived before she'd been bought by old Deihl. Like most town folk, I had mixed feelings about field slaves. They seemed ignorant, passive, backward; yet I was drawn to them inexplicably as if toward a dream I had forgotten and was trying to remember. There were almost thirty Africans at Green Gables, and they usually knew the truth of things, since the plantations were on the "peavine" that didn't pass through town. Like a fool, I was as excited by the horse as by the raid, but Cricket soon set me straight. "Once we get freedom," he said, "then we'll have all the horses we want." It began to dawn on me, that the fighting in Harper's Ferry had some purpose besides making the white folks angry and providing me with a little excitement. "I saw them this morning," I said. "Honest. They were walking into town, all with guns, and one of them . . ." "Hush," Cricket said, rapping the top of my head with his big knuckles. "Learn to keep your big mouth hushed up." I almost cried, he hit so hard. Cricket was three years older than I, and when you're twelve that seems like a century. Cricket was my cousin; he was my mentor, my secret idol, the big brother I'd never (I then thought) had. All the black folks were talking about the raid anyway, so I didn't see why I couldn't. There was a granny woman at Green Gables, and she said that God would send a sign of deliverance, a fire on the mountain. Sure enough, as soon as it got darker we saw it, blazing like a star that had come down and landed right on top of the ridge. All the talking stopped. All you could hear was wood and leather hinges creaking and children being hushed as everybody came out of the cabins and stood there watching, watching, watching. "Fire on the mountain," the granny woman said. "They up there sharpening they swords." Then she said that word again: *freedom.* It had a shivery ring to me, and I wasn't sure I liked it. I was afraid of granny women anyway. I told Cricket, and he told me to hush up again, then put his arm around my shoulder as if to apologize, and we stood there watching. I was nervous; I was afraid the white folks would see us and know what we were thinking. I looked behind me to the big house, but the curtains were all drawn. The granny woman must have seen me look around, or maybe others had done the same. "They trembling just like in the Bible," she said. "Trembling just like in the Bible." The fire blazed on, and finally I went home . . .

July 25, 1859
Miss Laura Sue Hunter
Miss Colby's School
Richmond

Dearest Lee Little Laura Sue:

While I agree with you, that Marriage is a betrayal of both Love and Freedom, I don't agree about Latin. It may seem a dead language now, but Latin is the language of learned discourse everywhere, not just in Medicine, and as our Age of Science advances toward its Noon it will be read and written more, rather than less. Believe me, there are those who would remove it from a young lady's curriculum. Do not make their work easier.

I'm glad you liked the poems I sent. I'm not surprised that your teacher prefers Milton to Lord Byron. You must hardly expect one whose job it is to keep you in a condition below that of Man, and above that of the Slave, to commend to you those whose calling it is to show you the very Stars. I say this to encourage, not discourage, your studies; for while Miss Colby's is not Harvard, it will afford you some knowledge, and while our father has many old-fashioned ideas, he is at least enlightened enough to educate his daughter, and that much can't be said of many of his generation.

I can appreciate the Excitement there, but no, I do not regard Brown as a Great Satan, nor do I think it is the end of the world. Do you not think it only Just, that the Slave, who has such willing oppressors, should also find willing friends? I'm afraid, however, that Brown will pay dearly for his boldness and, yes, humanity when the army brings him down. I share these Sentiments, of course, with none in the family but you.

Your loving brother,
Thomas

Grave robbing! Brown and Tubman left behind no wounded, but four dead, who were ignorantly and drunkenly abused and mutilated, then buried in a common grave in the mud of the sycamore flats near the Shenandoah. A week later the graves were robbed. The story whispered around was that some among the black folk had given them a proper heroes' burial. Well, that was not to be tolerated; the local authorities finally had something they could get their teeth (such as they were) into, and on the testimony of an ignorant "house nigger" called Jameson Jameson, arrested Granny Lizbeth at Green Gables and carried her into Charles Town caparisoned in chains. They tried to make her walk, but she wouldn't, so they brought her in a wagon escorted by six militiamen in matching outfits on horses with matching Hall's pattern muskets. It was quite a show for a 120-year-old woman. Mama all but tied me to the stove, but since Deihl needed me in the stable and was too busy to keep track of me, what with all the journalists and railroad men in town, I managed to get to the courthouse twice on the day she was tried. I watched them bring her in, and I watched the crowd outside the courthouse when it was all over. White folks had come from miles around, and one of them called out the proceedings from the courthouse door to all those who couldn't fit into Charles Town's tiny courtroom. You have to understand that these Virginians had never seen an African in a courtroom before; it was as unusual to them as trying a horse, and the fact that it was happening at all was an indication of the utter strangeness of things since Brown's raid. Well, Jameson Jameson was brought in but now said he didn't remember anything. The crowd in the courtroom booed. The prosecutor slapped Jameson, the judge admonished the prosecutor, and Jameson cried, and the crowd in the square laughed and ate fried chicken. As for Granny Lizbeth, they had three lawyers against her and only one for, but still she lost (as that old joke goes). After a one-hour trial she was found guilty of defacing a Christian grave (Christian, since two of the four dead were white men: I have always fancied that one of them was the boy

I saw on the road) and sentenced to a public whipping, the first in this part of Virginia in almost twenty years, although in the more elegant Tidewater such traditions die more slowly. Well, Granny Lizbeth, who was approaching 120 (she claimed, and we believed such things in those days) and had even less in life to fear than the rest of us Africans (though mostly we did not know it yet), bared up her yellow teeth (the cryer said) and threatened to call up the "very fires from Hell" if any "man, jack, or devil" so much as laid a hand on her. The judge, looking over his shoulder, suspended her sentence "on account of her advanced age and decrepit condition" and sent her home in the same wagon, without the chains. She rode out with her chin in the air like a conquering hero, and no wonder. A few of the white folks in the crowd booed and hollered, but most were dead silent: like the judge, they were looking over their shoulders; like me, they were afraid of granny women. Such was the state of mind among the whites the first week after the raid. Scared but angry. Angry but scared. Governor Wise of Virginia said the question of the outlaws up on the mountain was a federal matter, since it had been a federal arsenal that had been raided. President Buchanan said it was a state matter, since the raiders had never left Virginia. Wise said they had come from Maryland. Governor "Know-Nothing" Hicks of Maryland said they had committed no crimes in Maryland that he knew of. Buchanan pointed out that the sabotaged railroad bridge terminated in Maryland. Hicks said Buchanan (who was sixty-seven) was too old to know *with any certainty* one end of a bridge from the other. Etc. It felt like summer with a storm in the air waiting to cut loose. I kept looking over my shoulder, too, like the judge, but I was looking for something else, though I didn't know yet what it was. I helped Deihl with the horses twice a day and helped Mama with her kitchen, both of which chores had fairly doubled. The Harper's Ferry railroad bridge was still not fixed, and in the meantime eastbound as well as northbound trains were being routed through Martinsburg and Hagerstown, so Charles Town was getting all the traffic Harper's Ferry used to get, plus its own. Not the Charleston you know, great-grandson, the great Nova Africa seaport, but Charles Town, a dusty little Virginia county seat where the idiocy of rural life reigned unchallenged. The town was filled with government men, railroad men, newspaper men, plus the usual slave brokers, cattle buyers, and timber appraisers: most of them with horses, the rest needing them, and many of them, at least the lower elements, turning up at Mama's for cornbread and beans. The gentlemen and upper-grade government men ate at the Planters or at the Shenandoah in Harper's Ferry. John Brown had been good for business. Meanwhile the fire on the mountain burned and the black folks said nothing: little to the white folks and even less among ourselves. Later that week an ignorant "house nigger" named Jameson Jameson was found with his throat cut. The next week came Iron Bridge.

The Blue Ridge at Harper's Ferry is low but steep, tangled with laurel and stones, and split as if by a bread knife at the gap where the Shenandoah and the Potomac join together and slice through for the seaboard. After breakfast Grissom took Yasmin and Harriet for a tour. The museum's inertial car was big enough, but Yasmin could tell Grissom wanted to drive the university's, so she suggested it. It took them only twenty minutes to cover the steep streets of Harper's Ferry. There wasn't much to see. Floods and time had done what war had failed to accomplish, and except for the guests at the Shenandoah Inn, nobody lived below the Bolivar Heights—the bluff that edged the plain to the west. There were only the stumps and shells of brick buildings from the brief boom years before the War. The treasure of the town was not in its dank stone buildings but, as John Brown had so correctly noted, its strategic situation: cradled between two forked mountain rivers where they plunge through the gap in a mountain that was straight, smooth, and almost unbroken to the south, looking to Brown and Tubman like a spear pointing at the heart of the slave South.

There was nothing in Harper's Ferry to indicate its place in history, except the museum. Most of the John Brown memorials, Grissom told Yasmin and Harriet, were fifty miles up the Valley near Roanoke, his captured city, where he fought most of his battles, died, and, it was said, was buried on one of the peaks.

But no one knew exactly which one. "One of the interesting things about your great-grandfather's paper is the light he sheds on that subject." Grissom took a holo of his two visitors standing in front of the old engine house, where Brown had locked up his hostages, and they headed east for Charles Town.

The three of them sat in the wide front seat, Harriet in the middle. She seemed in a better mood, Yasmin noticed. Perhaps it was the shoes: they were no more colorful and the soles were still thick, but they had stretched a little up her ankles in a graceful curve.

Grissom stepped on the gas pedal, easing the big machine up to one hundred, enjoying the smooth rumble of the hydrogen-fired internal-combustion eight. The inertials, which ran on electric flywheel motors, made only a hum that barely changed in pitch or volume; with a top speed of ninety-five, they were steady, cheap, and safe. But unexciting. This magnificent antique roared like a corn picker when it was opened up.

"It's wonderful," Grissom said. "Do you drive it all the time?"

Yasmin laughed and shook her head. "The university keeps it for special occasions. I only got it because the motor pool manager's father was a friend of my great-grandfather's, and he convinced the school that it would be appropriate for the trip."

"And because she's afraid to fly," Harriet chimed in.

"I will fly. I just don't like to. I flew back from Africa."

"Gritting your teeth all the way," Harriet said.

"Still."

"I think driving is boring," Harriet said. "You can't see anything but bugs and sticks."

"Well, it's not boring to me," Grissom said, easing on up to 120. "I drove one of these in Chicago when I was a kid. I worked one summer for a millionaire out in Evanston. Speaking of the past, did you read the letters?"

"Most of them," Yasmin said. She remembered going to sleep with them on her lap. As always, when she remembered her recurring dream, her heart leaped up in her breast, as if someone had come for it: then it fell back, disappointed. "What a sad story," she said.

"I read some of them," Harriet said. "They're neat. But when does this Doctor Hunter meet granddaddy?"

"Keep reading, you'll see. Tomorrow morning I'd like you both to meet the woman who loaned the letters to the museum. I promised her I would bring you by."

"Tomorrow morning? But we have to be back in Staunton."

"It's the Mars landing," Harriet said. "We're going to watch it with Granny. Know why?"

"Of course he knows why," Yasmin broke in.

"I know who your father was," said Grissom. "And I know you're proud of him. Well, let me at least show you Charles Town while you're here."

*   *   *

37

Yasmin had been born and raised in Nova Africa, near Savannah. Like most n'African families, hers had its roots in the South but some of its branches north of the border, in the U.S.S.A. Most black people had moved south to the new nation after Independence in 1865; but many, like Leon's ancestors, had not. Yasmin had been to Virginia many times, but usually as Leon's wife (and then as his widow), always at the other end of the Valley near Staunton. She had never really known the Shenandoah, flowing northward like the Nile, where her own great-granddad had been born. He had left as a boy and she had no relatives living here now, as far as she knew.

Once, after her father had died, her mother had driven her through this part of the country, but that was twenty-five years ago, before the Revolution in the U.S., and Yasmin remembered only the filthy bathrooms and twisted faces of a country at war with itself.

It seemed more peaceful now, but still not prosperous. Maybe Africa had spoiled her. Even Nova Africa had seemed provincial and a little shabby after the grand plains, sweeping highways, and soaring cities of Zimbabwe and Azania.

Charles Town was a disappointment. Livery stables are as transient as clouds in the storm of history, and there was no sign of the one where Yasmin's great-grandfather had spent his boyhood. Yasmin had hoped Grissom would show them something more interesting than just the courthouse they had driven by the day before, but there was little to see. If Harper's Ferry had been left behind by history, Charles Town had been worked over: everything in the town looked new.

Socialist reconstruction, having patched up the ruined cities of the U.S.S.A., was finally coming to the little county seats.

From Charles Town they drove back west, but cut south before Harper's Ferry on a road alongside the Shenandoah. The west or Valley side of the river was gentle, golden, with wheat fields leading almost down to the water; but the east, the mountain side, was steep and wild. The river itself seemed wilder and rockier there, under the looming laurel thickets and jutting cliffs. Harriet looked up, trying to imagine what it was like for a band of men to make their way up, loaded with rifles and supplies and even wounded.

Ten klicks south of Harper's Ferry, Grissom seemed to find what he was looking for. He turned onto a growstone bridge near a small riverside compound consisting of three trailers and a broken-down welding shop and garage. He surprised Yasmin by stopping the car in the middle of the bridge and shutting off the engine.

"This is," he said, "or once was—Iron Bridge."

☆ ☆ ☆

August 10, 1859
Miss Laura Sue Hunter
Miss Colby's School
Richmond

Dear Laura Sue:

I was very sorry to get the word about John. He was Dear to us all but dearest and closest to you, and my Heart is with you at this time. I hear from Uncle Reuben he is to be buried in Baltimore, by Aunt Clare. I will be there when they bring him from the train. War is cruelest to the Innocent. Do not fill your Heart with hatred against those who mistakenly, but irrevocably, took his Life.

> Your loving and sorrowing brother,
> Thomas
> Philadelphia

☆ ☆ ☆

Yasmin got out of the car while Grissom began telling the story of the Iron Bridge Massacre to Harriet, who had of course heard it in school. "Served them right," she said. Yasmin agreed, she guessed.

Still . . .

Yasmin stared over the rail into the fast, unblinking, cold little eye of the river. She had always found the story fascinatingly cruel, almost like a fairy tale, even though it was true. At Iron Bridge the first effort to go after Brown and Tubman had met with a spectacular and horrifying defeat. A volunteer squad of Shenandoah Military Institute cadets, enthusiastic and foolish, swelled up with the arrogance of slave Virginia, had started up the mountain, led by one of their teachers with a special commission from Governor Wise (which he later tried to deny and hide). Not one had survived. They had been killed and laid out on the new iron bridge with their throats cut as a warning. That act of terror, Grissom explained to Harriet, had established in the mind of the South the seriousness of the revolt. It had given Brown and Tubman breathing space; it had discouraged volunteers. Yasmin had seen the old drawings from *Frank Leslie's Illustrated,* more precise and horrifying than any holo or photo could be, of the boys all arranged face up along the boards of the bridge. Throat up. The youngest of them hardly more than Harriet's age. Her horror and pity was not only for the boys, but for those to whom was given the work of slicing their pink, new necks, one after the other, fourteen in all. She looked down at the road and expected to still see the blood splashed around, beading up the dust.

Crueler still, they had let the teacher live.

"Cruel?" Grissom had sensed her mood. "Don't forget that these cadets were the scions of the old Virginia and Caroline slave-owning families," he said. "Black women wiped their noses all their lives. Black men saddled their horses and shined their boots at SMI. Maybe they didn't look so sweet and innocent to slaves."

"Brown and Tubman's men were mostly whites and free blacks then," Yasmin objected. "Slaves didn't join until later in the summer, up the Valley, nearer Roanoke."

"Still, the army had the political viewpoint of the slave," Grissom said enthusiastically.

It seemed an odd argument for a white Merican to be having with a black n'African, and Yasmin let it drop. She didn't exactly disagree. Anyway, it was part of building socialism; the Mericans were trying to rectify their view of history. There were still plenty of whites who in their heart of hearts (and some not so secretly) thought Brown was the Devil incarnate. As a historian and a revolutionary, straightening out the story was Grissom's job. And he was right: the killings struck a blow straight into the heart of old Virginia, wounding the myth of white invulnerability, the arrogance that would send armed boys after rebel slaves.

Still.

Did they cry for their mothers? Yasmin wondered, to herself. How did the knife feel in the hand? Heavy. Light. Like thunder and lightning together.

It alarmed and fascinated her that somehow her hand knew.

August 12, 1859
Miss Emily Pern
11 Commerce St.
New York

Dear Emily:

Thank you for your letter. My friend Levasseur is also encouraging me to go and hear Frederick Douglas

41

when he comes to Bethel Church next week, but it conflicts with a tragic and not unrelated event, a family funeral. I can no longer pretend to be personally unaffected by recent Events. I lost a young first cousin in the Massacre at Iron Bridge, near Harper's Ferry, who though misled and foolish, was much beloved by his Family. His name was John, my Uncle Reuben's eldest son. He was a student at Shenandoah M.I. He was exactly my sister's age, fifteen.

I must be in Baltimore when my uncle brings his remains Home.

I have heard so much that is noble about Douglas that even in my sorrow I am sorry to miss his appearance. I heard about it even before you wrote. Some say he was behind Brown on the raid, and others say he was against it. From what I have heard of his judgment and intelligence, I favor the latter. They say that Blood is thicker than water, yet I feel, truthfully, no vengefulness at my cousin's death, only sadness at the crimes that now stain the cause of Abolition. Revenge was never my strong suit, making me, I fear, a poor Virginian.

Meanwhile, here, the Copperheads are getting bolder. A colored man was beaten and killed two nights ago, and a church was torched, in retribution, no doubt, for Iron Bridge; which is precisely what I feared, the more dangerous elements inspired and unleashed. Violence has been sowed and will be reaped.

Douglas will be well guarded, I think. My friend Lev is urging me to plead exams and come to Bethel Church, but I would be far more than remiss to do so; Lev does not understand, I fear, the Southern family. My uncle and I are not close: he is my father's younger brother, and having moved North to enter law, he religiously sends his children South to be indoctrinated as Virginians. Thus the ironies of slavery: for I, the eldest of an eldest son, will inherit Mint Springs and its human chattel, which fate denied to him, a rabid enemy of Abolition. Meanwhile my father, in his illness, borrows regularly from his younger brother, who makes money hand over fist having been (to his profit) forced off the land into a profession. And I wonder will there be any slaves left to manumit when I come to my inheritance.

So I must to Baltimore. There were ten years between us and I knew John only as a child, which was, in truth, in understanding, all he ever attained. G.R.H.S.

Though I shan't hear Douglas, I expect to know of his words in detail, for if there's one thing I have gotten out of my almost four years of Medical school it's a plethora of friends with the ability to take sure Notes.

Any news of your plan? I hope you will continue to accept me as a true friend of abolition, of Hippocrates, and not incidentally, my dear Miss Pern, of Yourself.

> Your Faithful, &c.,
> Thomas Hunter, Esq, M.D. *(ad imminen)*

It was in the little things, like using a twelve-year-old to pick up dead fifteen-year-olds, that the South, even its less harsh masters like Deihl, showed its unthinking, casual inhumanity: the fact that we were not in their eyes human. It took three wagons to "gather the children home," (as the preacher put it, weeping) from Iron Bridge, and two of the wagons were Deihl's. I drove Kate. It's a rare horse and a common mule that can carry the dead without spooking. I have never forgotten the sight of those fourteen boys all in a row like ducks whose mama was the Gray Lady herself, their gray wool S.M.I. uniforms ruined with blood, being lifted one after another into the back of the wagon. No matter how gently they laid them down, the rusty springs shrieked each time. They didn't get to me, though, not like the youth I saw with John Brown on the morning road to Frederick. These were not boys like me: already dead, these were *things.* Plus, I knew they were not friends. Folks lined the streets of Charles Town when we brought them in. This was in the first shock, and nobody seemed mad. It was as if lightning had struck the town. Everybody seemed dazed. The men who unloaded the boys into the church kitchen, and the women who cleaned them up were mostly black, though the militia that stood over them at honor guard for two days while their families arrived was all white. Charles Town had never seen such fine families before, I guarantee. They came not only from Richmond and the Tidewater, but the Carolines, Charleston, and Savannah; as far north as Baltimore and as far west as the bluegrass of Kentucky. We didn't see them, of course, at Mama's; they were not your cornbread-and-beans type; but we kept their horses and traps at the stable and we fed their slaves in the yard, where Mama had fixed up a special "colored" kitchen. These slaves were first shocked and amazed at what had happened, and then curious and interested, all the time putting on a mighty show of grieving for the boys they had swaddled and raised. We slaves were the masters of grief's appearances, weeping for every tragedy but our own. It was the end of the week before I got a chance to slip out to Green Gables. I left Sees Her tied up behind the big house and found Cricket down at the slough. Cricket seemed not to like this new horse of mine; I do believe he was jealous, great-grandson. The trotlines were slow. Cricket was trading catfish to Mama and the cook at the Shenandoah as well. While we ran the lines, I described the line of bodies all with their throats opened like mouths, the howling of the wagon springs as they were laid in like cordwood, the buzzing of the flies. Cricket had to hear every detail. It was hours before we were done with the lines, and I wondered why we were going so slow. It was because Cricket had something to show me, and he was waiting for the moon to rise. Right after the moon came over the mountain, he took me out to a certain canebrake, to a certain little high piece of ground near the Shenandoah, and showed me four graves with four white crosses: each one decorated neatly with flowers and bottle glass and white conch shells, each with a new little pine tree planted on it, African-style. Here was the resting place of Brown's men. After Iron Bridge, it was like seeing the pretty side of death, the human side: for is burial not the most uniquely human of all our enterprises? Ants make cities and deer make roads, but only we of all creatures, in a tenderness and trustingness that would shame God if there were one, make graves. Cricket made me swear never to tell where it was. I went back looking for the spot years later, in 1895, thinking it should be made a shrine to the common humanity of all who died young so that Nova Africa might live; but it had all been swept away by the floods.

☆ ☆ ☆

Like all kids, Harriet loved to peel growstone: softer than balsa wood but stronger than concrete, it flaked off satisfyingly in thumbnail-shaped moons. She amused herself with the bridge rail (which would, of course, grow back smooth again) while the grown-ups argued; then she asked the question she already knew the answer to.

From here the road led across the top of the mountain, through Bear Pond Gap, Grissom told her. "Should we drive up there and have a look? Like your father," he said, "you're drawn to the high places."

That made Harriet grin and made Yasmin angry. She

couldn't tell if Grissom had said it to defy her silence about Mars, or to acknowledge it and make it seem more natural. Either way, his presumption angered her.

"Harriet, quit picking at the bridge," she said, and got into the driver's seat. It was, after all, her car. Sort of.

The top was a disappointment. The mountain was covered with white oak, maple, and hickory forest, turning beautiful in October colors; but there were few pines, no bare rocks, no feeling of height, even though they were at over a thousand feet. The mountain top was broad and flat where the road crossed and there was no view. Harriet got out of the car anyway, and stood on her tiptoes, as if maybe that last inch would reveal something.

Yasmin was just getting out of the car when, suddenly, two people crashed out of the brush at the side of the road. It was a man and a woman carrying backpacks topped with tents and bedrolls. Yasmin jumped back. With a wave the two crossed the road and disappeared into the brush on the south side of the road. Yasmin leaned back against the car, alarmed at how her heart was pounding. For a second, with their giant backpacks and white hats, they had looked like P.A.S.A. cosmonauts.

"There is a trail that runs along the top of the mountain, following the route of the Army of the North Star," Grissom was explaining to Harriet. Then he noticed Yasmin looking as though she'd seen a ghost: "Are you okay?"

She nodded.

"Hundreds of people hike it every year," Grissom went on. "Not just Mericans and n'Africans, but Canadians, Quebecois, Okla, Dineh, even Europeans. All the way from New England to Alabamb. The section from Harper's Ferry to here is especially pretty; it goes past False Fire, only a mile from here."

"Have you ever hiked it?" Harriet asked.

Yasmin scowled at her daughter as she got back into the car.

46

What a question to ask a one-legged man. But Grissom didn't seem to mind.

"All the way. As a boy scout from Chicago, forty years ago. Before the Revolution," he said. "Since then, not so much."

"Why don't you get a pseudo-leg?"

"The hip's all messed up, nothing to work it with."

"Can't you hike on crutches?"

"You probably could from here; you're already on top of the mountain. The trail coming up from the river is rough, though. I'll show it to you; you can see the beginning of it from the museum. What's that noise?"

Yasmin pulled the starter again.

Te-oonk te-oonk te-oonk.

"What's this?"

Te-oonk te-oonk. The engine fired, then there was a horrible clatter like dishes falling.

"Shut it off!" Grissom yelled.

Yasmin had already shut it off. "What was that?"

"I don't know. I think you lost your polarization."

"What does that mean?"

"Are we stuck?" Harriet asked.

"It means we switch over to planetary drive," Grissom said.

"Planetary?" Yasmin said, moving over and letting him into the driver's seat. "What's that?"

"Mother!" Harriet was already pushing, laughing. Yasmin got out and joined her.

"Planetary drive. Gravitational. In layman's words," Grissom said, "we roll down the hill." The car was rolling faster. "Luckily, the old guy in the house trailer by the bridge is an internal-combustion mechanic." Yasmin quit pushing and jumped into the front seat and slammed the door. "I know because I interviewed him for a folklore project last summer." Harriet jumped into the back seat and slammed the door. "Lewis, that was his name." They whooshed silently around the

47

long curves. "No, it was Leavis. No—" The road looped
through long halls of forest. "Angus. Elbow. Pelvis. Elvis.
That's it—" At the bottom of the mountain, after a sharp turn,
they fairly flew across the river on the bridge, toward the trailers in the sycamores.
"Elvis Presley Cardwell."

☆ ☆ ☆

August 16, 1859
Miss Emily Pern
11 Commerce St.
New York

Dear Emily:

I am writing to tell you that my plans changed, I went
to Bethel Church last night and saw the great Frederick
Douglass. Instead of a funeral I attended a Birth. Instead of a rain of tears, the Thunder of righteousness.
Even I, with my conservative (as you say!) Southern
ways, was moved. How like a lion is Douglass, a states-
man, a philosopher, and a fighter in one, and he has
done more in these two days to alter my opinions on
how to end Slavery (I had started to say On Slavery, but
my opinions on that Evil institution were long ago
fixed) than any other event or individual save, I must
own, perhaps yourself.

I went to Baltimore only to find that my Uncle had
accompanied his son's body South, to Mint Springs, our
farm in Staunton, saying that since John had died for
Virginia he must be buried there. So I returned to
Philadelphia in time to reach Bethel Church before
Douglass.

The notes I had hoped to get from others, I took

myself, and it was well that I did, since my friends were busy with other matters, as you will see. Here they are: transcribed for you from the Latin which has served me well these four years:

The Church was secured by some fifty abs, many of them students; some of them friends of mine and others, I am sure, friends of yours; and all armed with belaying pins from the docks. The greater number, perhaps half, were free Colored, most of them unionists from the seaport, but tradesmen and craftsmen as well. Some Irish stevedores as well. They all were led by a colored Teamster named Adam who is a stalwart of the movement here and apparently an intimate of Douglass, although he appears to be entirely innocent of letters. Over five hundred filled the church and an even greater number filled the street outside, since the whole town had cause to think that Douglass would speak on the subject of Brown's Attack, which as you must have heard by now he did. It was also known that the Federal Marshals had a warrant for Douglass since his name (among others) had been found among the effects left behind by Brown in the Maryland farmhouse from which he launched the assault that shook, not only the South, but the Nation.

If the Marshals and writ-servers were in the crowd, though, they were invisible and kept their peace, at least at first. Also, if the Copperheads and slave catchers had any Intentions they were not so bold, not that night, as to make them known. Certainly the street, filled as it was with the young, the hopeful, the working people, and half of them freed Colored, was a Republican and friendly crowd for Douglass; my friend and former French instructor Levasseur said of the crowd on the street that it looked like Paris in '48. Lev was one of the Stalwarts "on call," as he put it, in case of trouble, and in addition to the pin stuck in his waistcoat, he had tucked a LeFebre repeater in the top of one "Victor Hugo" boot; I caught only a glimpse of this as my friend is not the type, like others who were plentiful last night, to show it off as a vain augmentation of Manliness.

We heard Douglass approaching long before he arrived. It sounded like a storm coming through the mountains, the trees waving and sighing overhead before the wind and rain that move them are felt—this was the murmuring of the crowd outside the church doors. Everyone in the church stood as he came in the door and down the aisle, "Like the priest in the Church of Man," whispered Levasseur, who has a Jacobin turn of mind to fit his colorful waistcoats and high boots. The atmosphere was electrical.

The Colored minister, before introducing Douglass, alarmed I think by the mood and spirit of the crowd, called on God to fill our hearts with peace and love.

Douglass's first words might have displeased old Robespierre, but not of course John Brown (and Levasseur seemed well enough pleased himself), for they also called upon God, though not the God of the slave owners. —Almighty God— Douglass said, and if God didn't answer it wasn't because he didn't call out loudly enough. —Fill our hearts with love, but not with peace. Not yet. It is too soon for peace. Fill them rather with a tempest, with a storm of love for Man and a tempest love for Freedom. And also fill (here he paused and his voice dropped) fill our hearts with hatred (here the crowd including myself gasped!) Hatred for evil. Hatred for slavery, the foul enemy of man and freedom and love, slavery which degrades both subject and master—

A roar, half response and half applause, filled the hall, and Douglass held up his hand but could no longer stop it; he let it wash over him like a wave. He is a giant in stature as well as principle, six feet tall, wearing a pepper and salt suit of rather ordinary cut and a dark silk tie, no Jacobin, looking more like a banker than a revolutionist. Until he speaks: for there is no stiffness about his features. Just as his voice is like a chorus, his face is like a company of players, in which Humor, Tragedy, Wisdom, and Courage all are on stage at once. Though not exactly handsome, he is more distinguished in appearance than any Colored man I have ever seen. His head looks almost too large for his body, and his massy hair gives it a leonine look. He is the very opposite of stooped, if that be possible; he is bent a little upward, toward the sky, and his voice rolls out like thunder.

—There is much talk and speculation about a certain commotion down South— he said, to laughter and some cheers. —There are even those who rumor that my hand was involved— Here he studied his hand as if puzzled. More cheers. —There are rumors about another African, a woman who is well known and well hated by the slavers; a thief, this wicked woman, who regularly steals their property and then defies them to steal it back—

More tumult and cheers.

—There is talk of an old man, no gentleman he, but a rough-handed drover and tradesman, a man of God whose hands know both the Bible and the Sword, a white man well known to the slavers out Kansas way—

A regular tumult greeted these words. Douglass put

a stop to it by raising his hand, then lowered his voice and addressed the waiting silence:

—My friends, I did not come here to put all these rumors to rest. I come to encourage them. History will complete the roll call of the heroes of Harper's Ferry, but I will say this, and say it for a certainty— Here he paused again and peered out across the crowd as if looking for a face and then finding it. —Many of you were there. You, and you, and you (he pointed dramatically) in spirit, were there. The true lovers of abolition and liberty all were there, Sharps rifles in hand; or will be there, WILL BE THERE (he fairly thundered) ready to consecrate with willing blood a long-overdue and long-neglected bond of brotherhood with the most oppressed and despised of humanity—

After this last tumult died down, Douglass adjusted his tie, waved his hand, and seemed to call forth another, more thoughtful mood. The crowd was eager for more rhetoric, especially couched in such praise. But now he changed his tune.

—But not yet, my friends, not all of us. This consummation is yet to come. Some of us stayed home. Some of us, and I don't exclude myself, stayed home. Some of us— (and here I admit it, Emily, my ears burned) —love peace more than Freedom. Some of you whites would give the African his freedom, but not give him the gun with which to take it.

—Not Brown.

—Some of us Africans would ask for freedom, but not take up a Sharps and fight for it.

—Not Tubman.

—Not those of us who are with them tonight, either in spirit or On The Mountain . . . those of us who are True Abolitionists— (and here the word had a deeper and freer ring than I had ever heard before, bespeaking the end not just of slavery but of all darkness and ignorance and Hatred) —sons of Man and Reason, whether African or European, white or black, slave or free—

There was suddenly the sound of a scuffle outside, and a banging at the great church doors. With a signal from a Colored man, Levasseur was directed to the balcony, and at his gesture, I followed, though hesitating. Democratical as I am, I found it surprising to see a Frenchman taking orders from an African, and was reluctant to add a Virginian to this unusual chain of command. But Lev seemed not to notice my hesitation, and I had to either follow him or be left behind. In these speculations, and in moving upstairs, I lost the next few moments of Douglass's mighty talk. From the balcony we were looking down at the packed church and at Douglass in the pulpit, with a stout Negro armed with a staff at his either side.

The banging at the door continued, but he spoke over it:

—Think for a moment. What if John Brown had failed? What if he and his soldiers had been killed, or worse, captured? Oh, many a grand speech would then be made! Oh, what fiery denunciations of Virginia's cruelties we would then applaud! Brown and Tubman would be heroes and martyrs. Their men would be examples to us all of the willingness to sacrifice in the fight against slavery.

—But, alas, my friends, Brown has confounded us all. He has done more than sacrifice. He has succeeded. He has drawn blood. Just as in Kansas, he has drawn blood. In Virginia the old man has lifted his sword and drawn the very fire from the heavens, the blood from the earth. The enemy has fallen back in Terror; and not just the enemy; his friends as well, you see, have fallen back in terror. The old man has succeeded, and therein, my beloved fellow lovers of Liberty, lies the rub. For you see, not only does the slave owner need the slave, the abolitionist needs him as well; oh yes! Yes! Needs him to follow, to wait, to be patient. The old type of abolitionist, I mean. The peaceful type. But now his day is gone. Now to fight slavery we must do more than pass resolutions and make strong talk, and pray for the powerful to change their minds. Now there is a new factor in the fight. Before we had the familiar factors: the sullen slave owner, the fervent abolitionist, the wavering federal government, the slave groaning under his oppression; now we have a new factor, though none seem yet willing to call it for what it is—

Here his eyes flashed.

—Fire. There is a fire on the mountain. And Virginia can't put it out. America can't put it out—

There was such a tumult and a crying out at this as my poor words on paper can never express or even indicate.

—I am here to tell you, friends of Liberty, that there is, at this very moment, an Army of Liberation, an army of abolitionists, black and white; and already, freed African slaves, the heirs of old Nat Turner, the staunchest abolitionists of all, the most dreaded and feared; the Army of the Blue Ridge, the Army of the North Star— (and here was the first time I heard it so called) —high in the mountains of Virginia. This army calls upon and needs your wholehearted support, more than any one man's martyrdom or example. For it has changed, and will forever change, the nature of the struggle against slavery. There is now no going back, for us or for them.

—How can we support them? With our words. With our money. With our guns. With our sons. With our very lives. As they prevail, believe me, the struggle will spread to the North as well as the South, and we must prepare to face the same enemies they face—

I lost my notes for the next few moments, but there was a collection, and hats were passed around the interior of the church and passed to the altar overflowing with currency, even though the crowd was far from a wealthy one. I heard more scuffling outside, then the alarm of a shot, and the banging on the door renewed, but louder.

Here Douglass dropped his voice again, even as the pounding on the door increased in volume. His bodyguard, Adam I believe it was, tugged at his sleeve, but Douglass shook him off.

—As you may know, there is a warrant for my arrest as a confederate— (he said) —They flatter me. I am flattered because I know whereof I speak when I speak of the fainthearted, the hands that faltered— He held out his hand, then studied it himself as if it were a book. —Here is one hand that faltered. Black as it is, it faltered. Brown asked for my help, but I thought his scheme would fail. Our own Tubman knew him better. She knew the man, she knew the times, and most of all she knew our people. Now the two of them have my unconditional support, this hand is theirs, and if that be treason, if loyalty to my own dark, enslaved, suffering, and benighted people be treason to the U.S.A., so be it—

At this point, as if by a signal, the massive iron

fittings gave way and the door crashed down, inward. Two of Douglass's guards wrapped him in a cloak as if to make him invisible, in a scene befitting Shakespeare, while others leaped to their feet in the aisle. The panicked crowd meanwhile drew back into the pews. Six, eight, twelve federal marshals swarmed in across the fallen door just as Douglass was being hastened out of the pulpit, toward the choir door. The minister, an older Colored man, pushed through the aisle to try and calm the scene, but the marshals knocked him aside roughly. The crowd muttered angrily and there were cries. I counted twelve marshals and remember thinking they seemed severely outnumbered, and feeling both exultation and fear. I saw guns beneath their long coats, but there were no shots, not at that time. The crowd fell back and the marshals pushed forward for the pulpit.

Then full twelve of Douglass's men, the longshoremen, all black, filled the aisle, blocking them. Emboldened, but more slowly, others from the pews filled in behind them, placing a wall of men (and women) between the marshals and Douglass. Douglass himself stopped by the organ, drawing away from those who were hastening him through the choir door, to watch the drama behind him. The marshals ordered —Stand aside!— but the men in the aisle neither made answer nor moved. They seemed to be under the command of the giant Negro Adam, who stood in their midst, but I could not be sure; it was all done with flickers of eyes. They held long wooden pins from the docks.

The leader of the marshals called over them directly to Douglass; he waved a piece of paper without reading from it; perhaps like many U.S. marshals, he could not read the papers he served but committed his writs to memory. Douglass answered him, but with what, in the muttering and scraping, I could not hear. The marshal swore and pointed his Walker Colt at the great vaulted ceiling of the church, and—fired! Silence fell like thunder; the other marshals had opened their jackets and put their hands on exactly similar Colts. We all stood stunned; even Douglass froze like a statue at the choir door; all were stunned at the profanity of a shot in church: the only sound was the old preacher crying out—Oh, Lord— as if he himself had been shot, until someone, I think it was his own Daughter, shut him up. His Colt still pointed up, the head marshal stepped forward toward the line of Colored men. At this their leader, Adam, instead of falling back as expected, raised his wooden pin and pointed with it, in a great slow arc, like Moses with his Rod, to the balcony of the church, first to the right and then to the left, where I was standing. There was a steely rattle like snakes all around me, and the marshals stopped and looked up. I was as surprised as they to see guns drawn all around me, cocked and primed. Levasseur held his LeFebre across his nose like a dueling master; others, mostly Colored but with some whites mixed in, and several of them students I knew, across from me and behind me did the same; stalwarts with derringers and ancient horse pistols and new Colt revolvers all held at point, held the high ground of the balcony; there were perhaps twenty of them at most, but they looked like a hundred to me, and must have seemed a thousand to the marshal and his men, who froze with their hands on their weapons but never drew them.

The marshal slowly lowered his piece, then lowered its hammer.

Everyone else in the church stood stock still for a

breath, then two, then three. I counted them. I was standing with the armed men and without intending it I had become part of the tableau; at least the marshals looking up seemed to include me in it as we faced each other across a newly opened gulf in our common history as white men, a gulf John Brown had opened when he had drawn his sword in common cause with the black. This moment lasted no more than a minute, and no less than a hundred years.

Then with a flourish like Othello, Douglass was *exeunt* through the low choir door.

A low hubbub grew to a shout as the marshals backed slowly out the front door; the pews emptied into the aisles, the balcony into the galleries, the back door into the alley, and with the others, my heart pounding, I melted away into the night, which had fallen unannounced while we had been fighting our War in the Church.

It was the old Minister who was the only loser. For later that same night, Cowardice daring where Courage had faltered, his church was burned to the ground, probably by the same marshals who had been unwilling to take us on.

If I say Us, does that make me one of the Stalwarts? I think not; I still cannot imagine myself taking up arms (odd Virginian, I!), though, my dear friend and colleague, I definitely passed over a line in my own Understanding that night; the scales fell from my eyes, which is appropriate in Church, I suppose. Not about violence, which was the false issue, for that was never the question, slavery itself being the very perfection of violence; and not about my poor beloved South, for her corrupt true nature had long been clear to me. No, I understood that to end slavery we would have to be fighting the Nation itself and not just a section of it. Those were not Virginians that had come to take Douglass. We had to go against the might of America itself. This was what the slaves had always understood.

So, as you see, if Life is the great Instructor, I have been attending Classes. I only hope now that my family does not find out about this attendance, on the very night of my young Cousin's funeral; I have never hidden my abolitionary sentiments from them, but it is a fool that adds insult to injury. But I have, as I have said, only sorrows and no regrets. I remain, as always, your admirer and always devoted friend and colleague,

> Thos. Hunter, M.D. *(ad imminen)*
> Philadelphia, City
> of Brotherly Love

Aug. 16, 1859
Miss Laura Sue Hunter
Miss Colby's School
Richmond

Dearest Laura Sue:

I was sorry to say I was unable to attend our dear young Cousin's funeral, which was held in Staunton, you know, not Baltimore, our uncle saying that since John had died for Virginia he must be buried there. I would rather say, since it was Virginia that threw his life away, since it is a prodigious misapprehension of the Slave to think that he would submit to a Boy. I managed to get to Church on the night of the funeral, and my prayers were with you all.

> Your loving
> Thomas

☆☆☆

Socialism was good for teeth, and Elvis Presley Cardwell had a new set. He was sitting on the trailer steps when the car rolled in, as silent as a hummer, under his sycamores and stopped. It was the museum man with two colored women, one of them a child. But it was the car that interested Elvis.

"Haven't seen one of these in years," he said. "I don't work on cars no more. I don't call them little hummers cars. Sooner fool with a toaster. But this is different." He unpinned the engine cover, and Harriet and Grissom helped him lift it away.

He was the skinniest man Harriet had ever seen. He looked like a piece of string standing up.

He whistled approvingly between blinding white teeth. "This is pottery, children." He shut off the hydrogen on the firewall, connected a nearby battery into the "lube" circuit with jumper cables, and heaved on the flywheel with a broomstick. When the crankshaft turned, it sounded like the lid on a pickle crock being slid over. He nodded; the problem was the "oil" field. The reason the old pottery engines never wore out, Elvis explained to Harriet (who was the only one listening) was because the moving parts were separated by a magnetic field that kept the porcelain cylinder walls and the contraporcelain pistons a "fraction of a corn husk" apart. The circuit board that kept the field awake had popped a coil, and that's why the engine had rattled like a basket of pots. It shouldn't have even turned over, Cardwell said, much less fired. If they'd run it, they'd have killed it in less than a minute.

"Shame, too," he said, "to kill something that otherwise could live forever. Let's look under the injector board, right here, and see how old she is."

She was twice Harriet's age and less than half his own.

"I'd rather go to hell in a car than to heaven in a hummer," Cardwell said.

"I don't care what I go in," said Yasmin. "I just have to get to Staunton tomorrow, and I have to get that car back to Nova Africa in one piece."

Cardwell said the co-op wouldn't have a board this old; it would have to come from New York or maybe even Charleston. However, he just might find a board in a junked corn picker that just might work; there just might be one with a hydrogen pottery engine behind a dairy barn on the old Gentry place just this side of Winchester.

Leave the car and call in the morning.

It was getting dark by the time they got back to the Shenandoah Inn in a borrowed hummer. Yasmin called Charleston to tell them about the car. "Don't worry about it," the motor pool manager said. "Come back on the airship. We'll mail a board up, and somebody else can drive her down."

"No, I think it'll be fixed tomorrow," Yasmin said. "Besides, I have to stop back in at my mother-in-law's. I don't want her to have to watch the Mars landing alone."

Then Yasmin called Pearl to tell her they would be late.

"They're late too, honey," Pearl said. "Turn on your vid. There's a big storm on Mars and they can't go down. They're liable to be parked all of a week in orbit."

Oh no, Yasmin thought as she logged off and punched on the vid. She felt as if she was circling the planet with them; she wished they would go ahead and land so she could get on with her life. "Planetwide dust storm," the woman on vid was saying.

That settles it, Yasmin thought, scanning past. She decided to go on and tell Harriet she was pregnant, tonight.

While her mother was on the wire with Charleston, Harriet stood on the terrace outside the hotel room and scanned the mountainside with her eyes narrowed, trying to make out the trail Grissom had shown her on the map—the trail Tubman and Brown and their men had followed up the mountain on the Fourth, a hundred years ago, loaded down with weapons and cornmeal, shot and powder and dry beans, pursued by a lynch mob the size of a nation. All she could see were scarlet trees and dark green laurel, waving like pond weeds. There was a storm coming up, and the air was filled with leaves. Then suddenly there it was—the trail, revealed by three figures hurrying down the mountain on a long diagonal—day hikers, not carrying packs, trying to beat the darkness home. Just like in Dialectics class, the trail discovered itself when somebody walked on it.

Behind her she could hear her mother scanning through the vid. There was a story on about the Mars landing only hours away, but Harriet heard the finder scan past it, then double-click on eastern Kentucky quilts, "patterns as unchanging as the hills," as if anybody cared. Harriet wondered if they wrapped the dead in them, as the old-fashioned Gullahs on the Congaree River in Nova Africa still did. She bet they used pretty worn-out quilts.

She wished her mother would just let her father be gone, be dead, sail on, and quit worrying about him never coming home. Her grandmother said it was because Leon had never been buried. People were old-fashioned that way, she explained, they wanted to cover you up. But for Harriet there was nothing strange about her father sailing through space and never touching ground. She didn't want him covered up.

It was time to get home. Harriet had wanted to have her mother to herself for just a few days, before getting back to Charleston, school, friends, family, collective. But it hadn't been much fun. Her mother was distracted, vague, as far away as when she'd been halfway around the world, in Africa.

Maybe something had happened there. Maybe she had met a man and was going to get married. Harriet didn't even like to think about that.

She put one foot up on the railing and looked at her new shoes. It was neat that they were from space; she bet her mother wouldn't have gotten them if she had known. They had grown up her ankles, and when she stroked the high tops, they loosened slightly. They felt nice. The problem was, she had slept in them two nights and they still looked stupid: like gray house slippers with thick yellow soles.

She heard the finder scan back to the Mars story, double-clicking on it this time. The whole world was poised in orbit with the *Lion,* waiting on the storm that was scouring the canyonlands 1,200 klicks below.

When Harriet was at Vesey Youth Camp on Wadmalaw Island the summer before last, a woman from the Pan African Space Administration had made a special visit to show her the memorial plaque that the Second Expedition was going to put on Mars for her father. Harriet held it for a school picture. It was as light as a palm leaf, but it would last, the woman said, a million years. A million years. It was embarrassing because she had cried when they asked her to read it out loud.

"Harriet." She heard her mother's voice from right behind her, startling her. Then she felt her arms around her, as surprising and warm as sunlight from between clouds. "I have something to tell you. Don't look at me so worried like that, honey. Some good news."

☆☆☆

If Brown and Tubman are going to free the slaves, when are they going to do it? That was the question on most folks' minds as summer turned into the fall of '59. Of course, black folks and white were worrying about it from somewhat different perspectives. By September they had been on the mountain two months, and nothing had happened except for the disaster when the militia, and then the cadets, went after them. No slaves had been freed that anybody knew about. Meanwhile, federal troops—real troops and not just whiskey-tossers and hog-callers—were gathering in the Loudon Valley east of the mountain; and the slaves were waiting, watching, wondering, pondering. Freedom. What did it mean? Did it mean I had to live like the white folks? In spite of their nicer houses, I didn't envy them their mean, pinched lives. I envied the "free" black folks some, but not much. I even figured to be free myself someday, since Deihl had promised Mama and me our papers when we moved North. But it didn't mean much to me. There were plenty of "free colored" around Charles Town, and from what I had seen, a black man's freedom in a white man's world didn't amount to much. My real dream, which not even Cricket knew, was to go far away, beyond the mountains, away from the black folks as well as the white, away from Virginia, from America: and I imagined that somewhere over the rainbow (which I had seen once straddling the mountain like a bridge) there was a land where people lived in peace and harmony, didn't spit in the corners for boys to mop up; talked sweet to children; read books; didn't fight; didn't smell like wood smoke and horse shit. I know now it was Lebanon, a dream imparted to me along with reading by my homesick friend, the Arab—his idealized childhood Lebanon, mixed with every child's original dream of socialism, that genetic (I insist!) utopia without which there would be no actual socialism, with all its warts, for soul-hungering man. Some but not all of this sweetness I was to find in Nova Africa, some in Cuba, some in Ireland; but all that was still a lifetime away. Meanwhile, every night the fire on the mountain burned, and the question burned in folks' heads: If they're going to free the slaves, when are they going to do it? Then one night something happened that struck fire to my soul and settled forever all my questions about "freedom."

Cricket and I had been digging ginseng on the mountainside

to trade, a perilous business since the Shenandoah's main "sang"-digger, a poor white called Round Man, had claimed it all and was as jealous of his south slopes as a moonshiner of his springs. We gathered the stuff on Wednesday nights when he was at prayer meeting with his latest wife. I had been working late at Mama's, which was so busy since the hotel at Harper's Ferry was burned that we were serving cornbread and beans in the backyard in wooden bowls, and renting blanket rolls and a space in the barn for a quarter. Old Deihl was making money hand over fist. It put him in a good mood, and he was more willing than ever to let me ride Sees Her, since he was in a hurry to gentle and sell him. Cricket didn't like horses in general and Sees Her in particular, though, and I always left him tied up in the locust grove at the side of the home house at Green Gables, and true enough, he seemed to belong there: a finer-looking horse than what most of the white folks arrived on. Then I would cut on down to the cabins out back, giving out one of the many signal calls Cricket and I had.

This particular night Cricket and I were just coming back from our hillside piracy with a half a tow sack filled with Round Man's "sang" when we heard a bell ringing. It was the courthouse bell in Charles Town, almost three miles away. Then we heard another bell from Harper's Ferry, four miles to the north. One deep and one deeper. My first thought was to worry about Mama, for the bells were fire bells, but we found all the folks standing in front of the home house, on the high ground, muttering and milling around, looking off toward town. One old man called Uncle Tom said with a wide, sly grin: "It's Brown and Tubman. They burnt the courthouse. Brown and Tubman. Burnt the courthouse." He said it over and over as if it were a stick he was whittling. I asked him which courthouse, and how did he know; but at that moment we heard a lone horse, and a white man rode up on a lathered, sorry-looking pony

waving an old bowl-primed buggy pistol at the sky and hollering out: "They've burnt the church and the courthouse at the
Ferry, and they're a-coming this way. An army of 'niggers'
a-coming this way." I guess he thought he was Paul Revere
until he calmed down and realized who he was talking to, and
his face went cold. "Where's the white folks?" he demanded.
"Where's the old man?" he asked Cricket (referring to old man
Calhoun, who owned Green Gables). Cricket was never first to
respond when white folks asked a question; he had a way of
stepping back, out of his grin, so that he was gone but the grin
was still hanging there, almost visible in the air. It infuriated
white folks and they didn't know why. "They all in the house,
mister, sir," Uncle Tom called out. "Well, you all get back
where you belong, you hear?" our Paul Revere said. He
wheeled and rode toward the house with Uncle Tom and one
other following to take his horse. He hit the porch with his
boots clattering and started hammering on the door with his
gun butt, looking over his shoulder, until they let him in. Meanwhile Uncle Tom tied the horse to the porch rail. By now the
sky to the west, in the direction of Charles Town, was redden-
ing, and I could hear, or thought I could hear, thunder. Cricket
had stepped back into his grin and he shushed me: the thunder
was horses, far off, coming closer. We thought for sure it was
paddy rollers. All the slaves started melting back into the darkness, and Cricket pulled me back into the shadows of the big
elms, but I didn't need pulling. Horses meant white men, and
we knew they would be out for blood tonight if their courthouse
was burned. Then they rode into my life like absolute thunder:
for it was not the paddy rollers but John Brown's men. I looked,
but I could not pick out either him or Tubman. I learned later
that it was Kagi who led these early raids. There were sixteen
of them, mounted on fair-to-good horses, with one mount doubled. They all held identical Sharps carbines at the ready, blackened with soot so they wouldn't gleam; and they were all

masked. They all had black faces, but several had white hands showing through the laid-on soot. Oh, great-grandson, they were smart! They were bold. I had never seen so many black men on horseback, carrying such weapons. But the most astonishing thing of all was, they carried a flag—a new flag, an unknown flag. It was as big as a sail, and green and black and red in broad stripes, like Ahmad's of the Sudan or Garibaldi's flag of Italy (though I had never seen either at the time); all I knew was that it was not the American flag and the man carrying it was black like me. He held it in one hand on a long pole braced against his saddle horn, and it whipped in the wind he made as he rode it around the yard once, twice, fast, for all of us to see. Well, the slaves were coming out of the shadows now! We heard the windows scraping shut in the house behind us while we slaves gathered in the yard at gunpoint; there must have been twenty of us in all. I've never seen men and women so eager to be held at gunpoint, even fetching their children for the honor. The horses stood stamping and blowing in the dust while the rebels sent two of us out back with a rider to empty the smokehouse; it was the end of summer, and all they found were two of last year's hams (which the slaves had neglected to steal themselves). Somebody else came up with two sacks of yellow cornmeal. We only heard one sound from the house—a window scraping slowly open. In a flash an abolitionist turned and fired; a bullet whined off the slate roof, and the window slammed shut again. No more was seen or heard from the home house. Brown's men were all silent except for one African who barked out orders and made no attempt to explain their actions. I understood right away that they were robbing us at gunpoint so none of us could be accused of helping them, protecting us not just from the whites (who were too scared to be watching anyway) but from the traitors among us. They demanded horses, and Uncle Tom delivered up Paul Revere's pony without hesitation. I admit I hesitated for a moment, but only a moment, before I went to the locust grove and pulled Sees Her from the shadows; and without a tear (those came later, on command, for Deihl and his belt-whip) I handed the reins to the rider who was doubled up, who obligingly held a Sharps in my face. Then he did the strangest thing: he bent down and his rifle touched my cheek, like a cold little pat, and I burst into tears! Cricket thought he had hurt me and pulled me back angrily, cocking his fist and swearing at the man. But I wasn't hurt; I wasn't scared. The man behind this rider was wounded; he held his side and groaned as he slid off the back of his mount, and Uncle Tom helped him onto Sees Her. I patted his long old cold nose fondly and backed away, never to see him again. He was killed at Signal Knob. Then they were gone. I don't remember them riding away, but I remember their hoofbeats and someone shouting, "Fire!" Folks were banging on the door of Green Gables while others milled around in the darkness, confused. Somebody in the house was firing shots at the sky out a window while a few shadowy figures threw hay bales against the smoldering woodshed at the side of the house. "Good Lord, Miss Ann, they set the house afire!" It was burning (though it was to be put out and didn't truly burn until later in the war). It wasn't Brown's men who had started the fire, though of course they were blamed. Equally characteristic of the confusion of the times was that, collectively at least, the same Africans who set the house on fire, helped put it out. Cricket was shaking me by the shoulders: "Did he hurt you? Did you see those guns? Did you see that flag? Are you crying 'cause they took your old horse?" It wasn't an old horse, I said. Tears that I could not understand until decades later were streaming down my face. I had seen freedom and, yes, great-grandson, I wanted it. Bad. Though I was only twelve, youth and age drink from the same deep pool, and I knew then, as now, the sorrow in the heart of joy: I knew that I was saying good-bye not only to my horse but to my mother and my childhood as well.

I rode off with those horsemen, and I'm riding with them still.

☆ ☆ ☆

One of the goals of the U.S.S.A.'s second Five Year Plan (1955–60) was to reduce dependency on Canadian and Menominee small grain, and much of the former pastureland in the northern Shendandoah was golden with wheat. The valley opened out between Charles Town and Martinsburg, and it was like setting out on a golden sea.

"It's beautiful from an airship," Grissom said.

"Wouldn't know," Yasmin said.

She had called, but the car wasn't ready. Afternoon for sure, Mr. Cardwell had said. Since they had to wait around all morning anyway, Grissom was driving her in his little hummer to Martinsburg to meet Laura May Hunter, the owner of the Hunter letters. Harriet had stayed behind. To sleep late, Yasmin said. And to read.

"And watch vid?" Grissom ventured.

"I guess. The dust storm on Mars will be all over the news today. At least it will hold things up so we can get to Staunton, and Leon's mother won't have to watch the landing alone. I suppose you think I'm totally reactionary and neurotic for never talking about it."

"Not really," said Grissom.

"Well, I am. I guess."

"I've been thinking about your situation," Grissom said. "It's hard enough to lose somebody, but when they're famous like that, you lose them but they're not gone. They're everybody else's. They've been expropriated, nationalized."

Yasmin laughed grimly. "I never thought of it like that. Isn't that sort of a weird way to look at a relationship?"

"I bet it's different for Harriet, though," Grissom went on.

69

"I bet it doesn't hurt her as much as it does you. It would probably do you good to talk about it yourself."

"I know," Yasmin said. "Actually, she and I had . . . a little talk last night."

Unlike Harper's Ferry silently commotioned by the shadows of airships sliding overhead, Martinsburg wasn't on the way to anywhere. The only things sliding over were clouds. It was a flat, bustling little city north of the Potomac, where the valley widened out so that the mountains weren't visible on either side. Yasmin found it ugly. Socialism to the Mericans apparently meant that the new buildings should be all the same size, shape, and color, like soldiers in uniform; and in Martinsburg many of the buildings were new. In Nova Africa that phase had lasted only a few years, but now even those turn-of-the-century buildings seemed charming in their naïve sameness.

Maybe I'm just homesick, Yasmin thought. She was flooded with a sudden desire, almost frightening in its intensity, to see her little wood-frame ochre house on the canal in Charleston.

They stopped to top off the battery, and Grissom phoned the old lady's house. Yasmin noticed that people down here talked a little more like Grissom and a little less like her mother-in-law. The African-softened accent of the border was noticeably beginning to give way to the harsh Northern twang.

But Laura May Hunter still lived on the border. The first thing Yasmin saw when the uniformed day nurse let her and Grissom into the little house was a tinted picture of Abraham Lincoln on the wall.

Lincoln was a Whig, backed by U.S. capital, who had organized a fifth column of Southern whites to support an invasion of Nova Africa in 1870, right after the Independence War. If the whites couldn't keep the slaves, they at least wanted the land back. Though the invaders had been routed at the Battle of Shoat's Bend without crossing the Cumberland River, "One nation indivisible" had become a rallying cry for white nationalists on both sides of the border. The next five years, 1870–75, were as close to a civil war as Nova Africa was to see. When it began, the new nation south of the Tennessee River was 42 percent white; when it ended, it was 81 percent black. In the U.S., veterans and descendants of the "Exitus" formed the racist backbone of the rightist movements for years: in the Bible Wars of the 1920s, the Homestead Rebellion, even the Second Revolutionary War of '48. In Nova Africa the whites who embraced (or made their peace with) socialism were called "comebacks"—even if they had never left—and Lincoln was no hero to them; but before his body had even been cut down in 1871, he had become a legend among the border whites in Kentucky, Virginia, and parts of Missouri.

Apparently he still was.

Yasmin pointed the picture out to Grissom, who nodded, then shrugged. "The Lost Cause," he whispered.

Following Grissom, who was following the nurse, Yasmin entered a dark parlor and sat in one of three floral-print chairs while the nurse went out with a wheelchair, one of three parked in a row in the corner. "She doesn't have the same politics as her ancestor," Grissom whispered. To say the least, Yasmin thought, beginning to wonder what was the purpose of this visit. The room was like a shrine to white supremacy. A painting showed Andrew Jackson strutting under a twenty-six-star flag across a field of dying Creek and Cherokee. On an end table several books sat upright between harp bookends: the *Holy Bible;* Palgrave's *Golden Treasury*; Walker's *Sea to Shining Sea*; Emerson's lament for a lost America; *Gone With the Wind*; and one title that caught Yasmin's eye, *John Brown's Body*. She pulled it out far enough to see a lurid picture of a hanged man on the cover, then shoved it back just as the nurse wheeled her patient into the room. Above the lumpy sofa another Lincoln, this one a holo, stared down with big, mournful, calculating hound eyes.

With the burning of the Charles Town courthouse, the waiting was over, or so it seemed. Everybody seemed relieved, especially the white folks. The war was on. Another plantation house was torched the week after Green Gables; and this one burned to the ground, the slaves not so foolishly putting it out but, Cricket speculated (acting this out), blowing on it. Another, two days after that. As the Shenandoah was not serious plantation country, this pretty much exhausted the opportunities. The slave market that was burned at Sandy Hook wasn't really a market but a holding pen for "beaters" heading up the Potomac from Washington and south along the Valley road, to the cotton and hemp country of the south and west, where slavery was big business. Meanwhile, the town was filling up with volunteers, adventurers, contractors, and newspapermen waiting to see what the government was going to do and how they could turn a dollar off it. All of them were white, all were men, all were armed, and all of them were full of strong talk. Around the kitchen and the stable, I heard their rumors, their boasts, their threats, and even (reading between the lines) their fears. None of these men was eager to go up the mountain after Brown. Not after Iron Bridge. They were all waiting on Holliday, the head of the Virginia militia, to arrive from the Tidewater. The private talk (for a stable and tavern boy heard lots of private talk) of Holliday's agents, who were already in town arranging provender, was that these over-the-mountain fur-hat hillbillys didn't really know how to deal with "niggers," as white folks felt free to call us in those days. The fur-hat hillbillys let them talk. Though the militia, press, government, and army alike, stayed at the Planters or the Potomac, those who weren't "on found" tended to eat lunch at least at Mama's. It was cheaper and better. Everyday the big parlor was filled with a wild mix of white men, and the backyard, under the catalpa tree, with colored. Mama gave all the same fare: cornbread and beans, greens and hamhocks too fat for eating (a hamhock in those days, great-grandson, would flavor a week's beans; they weren't your skinny wartime hams), chicken, pork, squirrel and dove in season, rabbit and catfish, all the game and fish brought from her extensive network of slave and free black entrepreneurs. Mama had her partialities, though, and she would often give me a plate of pigeon breasts or sweet little squirrel hearts to set down near a certain favorite, always a preacher, and always colored. (We didn't get white preachers whatsoever; I doubt Mama would consider them real preachers anyhow.) Mama was in her element, serving rough men strong food and making money: for though she was a slave, she managed all of the old German's money. She liked a crowd as much as Deihl shunned society. Her warmth in this crowd was in contrast to her brooding silence in private. I found her, my own mother, proud, cold, shy, and mysterious; she seemed to come alive around others, but alone she was remote and distant. I regretted being an only child almost as much as I regretted slavery, though I knew the two were linked; Mama had told me that the reason she'd been sold to Deihl was because she could bear no children after me. I think now, looking back, that the lonely life of semifreedom in town, in a white man's house, killed something in her by taking her away from her people. But she had wanted it; she managed both our lives and was a slave in name only. Those were strange days, great-grandson. Two countries were fighting a war by night but eating out of the same pot of greens by day. In fact, the whites seemed positively friendly that August, thinking, I'm sure, that the "niggers" who weren't up the mountain liked both slavery and them. This particular one of their illusions didn't survive the winter. The black folks, especially those in the town, seemed more mistrustful of one another than of the white folks in those first months of the war. Maybe it was the affair of Granny Lizbeth that did it. All the talk under the catalpa out back was of mules and weather and food, as if there were no such thing as the fire on the mountain, no army of abolitionists burning plantations and setting slaves free. I used to study those dark faces and wonder: did they really believe nothing had changed? Or was it part of the centuries-old mime the African played for the whites and, ultimately, for ourselves as well. We kids were going through our own changes. Since the raid, and especially since the night I lost Sees Her and found the flag (as I think of it), Cricket was more brotherly and less ornery than usual. He didn't pick on me and boss me around like before. Meanwhile, the few friends I had had among the white kids in town, such as Sean Coyne, were gone. I didn't see them anymore, not after Iron Bridge, not after the courthouse for sure. And I didn't miss them either, except for Sean. I later learned he was killed at Roanoke toward the end of the war; he died with me owing him two taws and a clay, which I would gladly put on his grave today, could I but find it. I was busier than a one-armed blacksmith, since I had to deal with the mules and horses (doubled in number) morning and night, and dinner from eleven to three. I got out of washing up, though, since Mama had hired two girls. War times are flush times in the livery business. Deihl was off almost every day in the Valley buying up horses and contracting for hay. I missed the old man around the stable. Except with Sees Her, or any troubled horse, he was a far better hand with horses than I, since he genuinely liked and understood the beasts, and I was always faking it, finding them the only living thing dumber than wood. With Sees Her gone, all I did was throw them hay and water. I never took time to rub them down or look at their hooves, though the militia and government men didn't mind and seemed to care as little about their animals as I did. These were the first strange days, great-grandson, of the war we didn't yet realize was a war.

Then late one afternoon while I was watering the horses I heard a Tidewater voice say the word "war" as if it had three syllables, and I froze as still as a deer. I was in full view of two men across the barn, but if you have ever been a twelve-year-old African in a white man's country, you know what it is to be invisible. Just to make sure, though, I backed up between two horses and started rubbing them down, which would have alarmed any more intelligent animals, since I had never laid on them with a brush in my life. Under their bellies, far off under the hayloft, I could barely see two pairs of English-style boots facing each other, but barn sound is funny, and I could hear their voices as if I were standing next to them. They were planning an ambush that night out the Old Quarry Road, where they had intelligence that Brown's men were coming down nightly for supplies. From the amount of tack and horses, I figured their force was about thirty men, as big as Brown's whole army! When Deihl came back, they contracted for all our horses, leaving their own behind. I suppose one of the benefits of being in the government militia is that you subject a rented horse to fire and not your own. I was until almost dark getting the tack and mounts together; meanwhile I was burning inside. I had to tell someone. The only person I could trust, who would know what to do or who to tell, was Cricket; but he was three miles away at Green Gables, and it was already getting dark. I was still trying to decide what to do when Mama called me to help with the dinner spread. Something told me not to answer. It was dark by the time I got to Green Gables, out of breath all the way, and to my dismay Cricket was gone; running about everywhere, I checked down by the slough and out in the woods. There was no one else I trusted to tell. Cricket trusted the old granny woman, but I didn't trust her or anyone. Cricket

75

had said the fire two weeks before had cleared things up between those who poured water on the fire and those who
"blowed on it," but this didn't help me, since I didn't know who
had taken which side. Besides, things had changed. Nobody on
the plantation seemed to want to talk to me, or I to them. I
sneaked home on foot, heartsick, hating all the slaves; and
surprisingly, got neither a scolding nor a whipping from my
mother, who thought I was coming down with something and
sent me to bed. I crept on up to my corner of the loft, and maybe
I *was* sick: I went right to sleep. It was almost dawn when I was
awakened by the sound of horses. They didn't sound right. I
peered out through the crack under the eave I had opened up
for summer and saw a big bay eating Mama's roses, his head
not five feet from mine, nosing the roses, them gobbling them
down. He was riderless, and his saddle had slipped down under
his belly, and his back was smeared with blood. Two other
horses came up, whickering into my little field of vision, one of
them dragging one leg. I heard white men hollering far away.
The back door slammed downstairs, and Deihl hopped into
sight like a chicken, pulling on his filthy old pants, grabbing at
the horses. It was like a scene from Hell. The ambush had been
ambushed, and the horses had come home. Six men had been
killed and twice as many wounded. The two Tidewater gentlemen rode in on one mount, one of them shot in the arm but not
excited about it, I'll grant him that: those Virginia slavers were
cool customers to the end. I worked at cleaning up the horses
while Deihl shot two. I always wondered why he spared me
that, but not the gruesome work with the boys. It must have
been hard on him. Through the day the news got worse and
worse as the wounded came back. Worse for them, the whites,
that is. I looked at black folks with a different eye by the evening
of that long and bloody day, bloodier for Deihl since he lost four
horses—two of which, ironically, the U.S. government still
owes me for, since Mama was freed before she died and left her

half to me. I was excited. It was clear that the raiders on the mountain had more friends—and more effective friends—than me. I delivered a plate of cornbread and side meat and beans to Mr. Pleasance up at the Planters Hotel that night, and instead of cuffing me, as he did when he was mean drunk, or giving me a nickel as when he was generous drunk, he had me set it outside the door. Then he slid a nickel under the crack. For me that nickel sliding was the true beginning of the war.

☆ ☆ ☆

Laura May Bewley Jenks Hunter was a tiny little woman like a china figurine: bone-white, covered with a web of fine wrinkles like crazing. She must be ninety, Yasmin thought, although she knew she was a poor judge: white people looked old to her at sixty. The old woman peered at her through huge glasses, then touched her hand. Satisfied that this visitor was real (as if perhaps she had plenty of the other kind) she settled back into her wheelchair and smiled. When she smiled, powder cracked from her face and fell into her lap like snow from a shaken tree.

Yasmin told her how much she'd appreciated reading the letters. It would have seemed rude to have said "enjoyed."

Mrs. Hunter explained that her mother had been the sister of Dr. Hunter. All the letters had come from her, since Dr. Hunter had left no heirs. Yasmin had figured out that much; her question was, how had she gotten hold of the "Emily" letters? Even though it had all taken place a hundred years ago, Yasmin was reluctant to ask. It seemed like prying.

"My father was a Bewley, of the Lynchburg Bewleys, and my husband was a Jenks, you know, but when he died I changed my name back to Hunter. The Bewleys were nobody in particular, and the Jenkses were nobody at all. You know when you get old, dear," the old woman said, "the past seems closer than the present."

77

Black folks called you "honey," and white folks called you "dear": Yasmin had noticed that as a child, and it still was true. She herself had called Harriet "honey" last night when she had told her she was going to have a baby brother. Brother? Had she really said "brother"? Did she really think that? Did her subconscious know some secret her body hadn't yet revealed?

"Now looky here."

The old woman was opening a little cedar box she held on her lap; she pulled out an ancient, browned tintype.

"Here's my mother, Laura Sue Hunter, as a girl with her brother, Thomas Hunter, who wrote the letters. He left no heirs, you know."

She handed the photo to Yasmin, who studied it, looking for some sign of the young man who had heard Douglass thundering at Bethel Church; whose best friend was a Jacobin; who was in love (did he even realize it?) with a Yankee bluestocking. But the picture was too posed and dim: a Southern belle standing next to a Virginia gentleman, both completely characterless, like holos of photos of drawings. She was a teenager made up to look like a woman; he was a boy in his twenties with an eager mustache, wearing a frock coat. They were standing in front of a photographer's painted backdrop of a columned house, Spanish moss and cotton fields stretching off into the distance, in a scene totally unlike the Great Valley of Virginia where they had lived. Yasmin's eyes were drawn back by the perspective, to the tiny stylized black dots bending down between the rows.

"She married a Bewley, of the Lynchburg Bewleys, but she was a Hunter through and through," the old woman said. "He, on the other hand—my uncle—he was what you might call the black sheep of the family. Wouldn't you call him the *black* sheep, Dr. Grissom?" She smiled, and another light avalanche of white powder fell into her lap.

"Of course, blood is thicker than water, isn't it, dear? You colored do hold to that, don't you?"

78

"I beg your pardon?" Yasmin sat up, startled, but Laura May Bewley Jenks Hunter went on as though hard of hearing:

"Did you enjoy the letters? You can keep them a few more days."

The old woman's fingers fluttering on the back of Yasmin's hand felt like a bird's claw. Yasmin let her pluck the picture back and put it into the box; then watched, curious, as she pulled one of the books from between the bookends.

"I want you to read this, dear," she said. "Just be sure and have Dr. Grissom return it with the letters." She squinted, and powder whitened the back of Yasmin's hand. "Which one is it?"

"John Brown's Body."

"Oh, yes."

September 11
Miss Emily Pern
112 Washington Square
New York

Dear Emily:

Herewith, the names you requested for the Medical assistance campaign. Though I am happy for you that you are going to Medical school, I am sorrier than I can readily say to hear that you are going to England. Friends are rare in this life; a woman friend rarer still. Trusting neither the times nor the mails, I send this, because of the names, by hand with my comrade and confederate Levasseur, whom I commend to your trust absolutely. I hope things at home with your family are well. I am soon off on family business myself, to Baltimore, where I am to present my sister at Harvest Cotillion, my father being presently too ill to travel. I don't look forward to the ceremony, although Laura Sue is a favorite, and makes one grieve for the young minds that are extinguished in finishing schools: another side of the human waste of slavery. I get regular reports from the South and can only say that people there are terrorized, and agitated, and bellicose, even with their closest relatives. I fear War. Will we meet again before you sail?

Yours &c., &c.,
Thos.

☆ ☆ ☆

"Now what am I supposed to do with this stuff?" Yasmin said, looking at the paperback and the letters on her lap as they were driving back toward Charles Town. "If the car's ready, Harriet and I are leaving for Staunton as soon as I get back."

"Leave them with me. I'll return them. That way she gets some company," Grissom said. Without taking his eyes off the road, he picked up the book and thumbed through it. "Now why did she give you this? That sly old devil."

"It looks gruesome."

"It is, in its way. You never read it? I wrote a paper on it in college. It was a bestseller in the 1920s. It's a border fantasy, a what-if."

"What if what?"

"What if Brown and Tubman had failed. What if the U.S. had won the war."

"You mean it's pro-slavery?"

"Well, not exactly," Grissom said. "Worse than that, really. It's a sort of a white supremacist utopia, mis-topia maybe."

"So if it's not about slavery, what's it about?"

"Empire. By the middle of the nineteenth century, slavery was about finished anyway," Grissom said. "Africans around the world were throwing it off. The real issue in the Independence War was land. Nationhood."

"So there's no Nova Africa." Yasmin riffled the pages. "Does Tubman hang too?"

"She's not there," Grissom said. "That's the trick the plot turns on. The idea is that instead of going on the Fourth as planned, Tubman gets sick. The raid is delayed until fall, October I think. Brown goes without her. Now according to the book—and in actual fact—Brown was more of a strategist than a tactician. Without Tubman he hesitates, takes hostages, lets the Washington train go through. You know, in real life it was Tubman who insisted on blowing the Maryland bridge and cutting off the train. Anyway, in the book they don't blow the bridge; they get trapped in the town, captured, and hung as traitors."

"So we have John Brown's body and no war."

"There's still a war. It's just not an independence war. It's fought to keep the old U.S. together rather than to free Nova Africa."

"So who wins?"

"The North. Lincoln," Grissom said. "In this book, he becomes President and the war is started by the slave owners, who are trying to set up a separate country—like Nova Africa, as a matter of fact, on pretty much the same territory . . ."

"Clever."

"But a slave country, run by the slave owners."

"They already had that, for all practical purposes," Yasmin said.

"They were losing it by 1860, or at least thought they were. They didn't want another Kansas. Anyway, in the story the North fights to keep the South in the Union. And they do. They win."

"And we lose."

"And how. Listen, this book was a bestseller in the U.S. in the 1920s. Lincoln's a big hero; so's Lee . . ."

"Lee?"

"He leads the army for the South. He plays the good loser, the Virginia gentleman, generous in victory, gallant in defeat, shaking hands at the end—all that."

"Amazing," Yasmin said.

"White right prevails; the slave owners keep the land, even get more. The slave system is modified so that n'Africans end up as serfs; or worse, as a sort of landless nation packed into the slums of Chicago and New York for occasional servile labor."

"No Nova Africa."

"Afraid not, comrade. One nation indivisible—it's old Abe's dream, and your nightmare. You all don't even get a hundred acres and a mule."

"Mis-topia, dystopia, wishful thinking." Yasmin put the book back on top of the dash. Then she picked it up again with two fingers and looked at Grissom sideways. "That sorry old woman gave me this to insult me, didn't she?"

Grissom looked surprised. "Oh, I don't think so. She's not *mean.*"

"You think. You wish. Sure she did. 'You colored,' she called me. I thought she was just senile."

"She is, she's just muddled; hell, you heard her, she thinks I'm a doctor."

"You're blind, Grissom. That sly, old pale thing. This is her revenge." Yasmin thought about throwing the book out the window, into the sea of yellow wheat. Instead, she turned it face down on the dash.

"And even worse," she said, turning back to Grissom, "here you are, a revolutionary, courting these old renegades just so they'll leave their papers to your precious museum."

Grissom blushed angrily. "That's absolutely not fair! It's not true. Do you want me to be rude to some poor old lady with hardening of the arteries? You know these aristocratic southrons."

No, I don't think I do, Yasmin thought. Don't think I want to. How close the past looms, circling the present like a dead moon, lifting slow repetitious tides on the living planet. She hoped the car was ready. She was tired of these white folks and their ancient craziness. Luckily, when they pulled into the shed at Iron Bridge, the car was ticking over with all its old elegance, and Elvis Presley Cardwell was standing proudly beside it, his wide grin showing off his new teeth—made of the same material, Yasmin realized, as the engine he admired so much.

After the Battle of Quarry Road, as we called it (the white folks called it the Quarry Road Massacre), Wise and Buchanan apparently settled their differences, for two days later a train filled with marines and horses came from Washington, D.C., across the newly repaired railroad bridge, through Harper's Ferry, heading for Charles Town to occupy the lower Shenandoah. Another column came marching from Eagle, through the Gap, and a detachment stayed in the Ferry. Drums rolled and flags flew and horses and cannon marched by all day; and all the boys in the town turned out, colored and white as well. But things were changing. I had never had any problem with the local white boys, perhaps because Charles Town was a railroad town and there were so many "shanty Irish" and Germans, making it far different from the farm country to the south. Harper's Ferry was even more of a railroad town, with almost half of its population "free colored," so even the white boys who were inclined to mess with us didn't. I wasn't until much later to know what an unusual situation that was in the South. Brown, of course, had known it all along. Cricket had derided me for these white friends, finding it childish (on the plantations slaves had friends among the white children only up until age seven or eight); and perhaps Cricket was right and I was hanging on to being a kid, even at twelve, through my Merican friends. At any rate, all that was changing: changing like the seasons as war, like winter, rolled in and we watched, shivering inside. Like an iron frost. You could have seen my breath that day, standing on the street watching the troops and cannon fill the town. I was very aware that the army was here to kill something hiding out (and I think the other black folks felt this as well) not only on the mountain, but inside my heart as well. So I was quiet; I feared it. The grown-ups cheered, but at first, for a time, the white boys were as silent as I was. It was strange how quiet they were, considering how much boys like soldiers. I think boys have more sense than they get credit for: I believe, great-grandson, they understood, for a moment, anyway, that with this war their childhood, like mine, was over with, and the season coming would be long and cold and mean. They got over it, though, and soon joined the grown-ups, who think about the future less clearly and less often: they all whooped and cheered and cast dark looks about at the few black faces, as if we were burned biscuits disgracing their table; I withdrew as soon as I could with honor, to watch the rest from the loft of Doug Bean's store. We Africans had an army too; I had even seen it. It seemed unfair that we couldn't have our own parade with drums and cannon and flags and horses rearing about. The commander of the marines was a West Point colonel named Robert E. Lee, who was also (and certainly not coincidentally) the scion of an old Tidewater family. Thus were here combined both the big guns of slavery: the federal government, with the accents and concerns of the Tidewater; and rightly so, since it was the Tidewater that created both slavery and, some say, the federal system, now both gone with the dinosaurs. I was impressed in spite of myself. Lee was the very original of the Virginia slave owner: tall on his horse, and short off it. I learned at lunch that day, and the next, that many of the "free" black folks were glad to see him and the federal troops, since the men in town had grown wild and mean since Quarry Road—the militia and the free booters, the Kentucks and Tennessees from over the Cumberlands. Folks hoped Lee would tone them down a little. But if anything, he made them worse. Now that they didn't have to worry about going up the mountain, they paraded around Charles Town drunk every night, cutting each other up, stealing horses, threatening "niggers," and generally making themselves obnoxious and dangerous. At "Mama's" (which is what Deihl called the lunch kitchen she ran for him), they watched their manners, but in the street I would be insulted or even threatened by the same low-grade hillbillys who begged for extra biscuits to slip into their greasy shirt pockets at lunch. A few days after Lee's arrival, they hung John Brown in effigy and horsewhipped an old deaf black man in Charles Town, a thing they would not, I think, have done before. In Winchester they tarred and feathered a Philadelphia newspaperman, even though since the latest "massacre" the Northern papers, even the most staunchly abolitionist, were no longer sympathetic. Both times the Federals stood by and watched, licensing rather than preventing such behavior. So now we were under martial law and there were American flags everywhere, though the troops only amounted to a detachment in each crossroads and a main force at Charles Town. That night of the day Lee came, I went out to Green Gables. I felt lonesome in town. I felt like seeing Cricket. Since Brown's men had ridden through and tried to burn the house, old man Calhoun had moved to town with the womenfolks; his son-in-law and his overseer stayed, but with the house boarded up like a fortress. The crops were laid by and there wasn't a lot of work to do. Green Gables was on the African "peavine," and the news from the east and down the Valley was ominous; there was talk of panic among the whites and of slaves being sold off South, to the new cotton lands in Mississippi, or worse, the hemp plantations in western Kentucky or the turpentine forests in Georgia, where men were cheaper than mules. There was other talk, too. One Green Gables slave whom I had barely known, a silent, grieving man named Little John, only recently bought, had gone "Up the Mountain" a few nights before. He was the first from Green Gables, and nobody knew what to expect. People said old man Calhoun was trying to collect the insurance, but the underwriters were maintaining that "insurrection and war" invalidated the claims. Meanwhile, the folks at the Gables hardly ever saw a white face (or a red one, as the besot Irish overseer was hardly "white"). I waited around for Cricket, then went looking for him. My hoot-owl call was answered, and I found him out in the graveyard behind the kitchen gardens. Cricket had a little brother who had died at birth, along with his mother, and Cricket left him something shiny or bright every week: a piece of bottle glass or creek stone, or even a toy. Cricket said this kept the child from crying; thus he was helping his mother in "Africa," as the slaves called heaven. Plus, he claimed his little brother's ghost brought us luck on our trotline, sang-digging, and other enterprises. I always found that little foot-long grave fascinating, festooned with glass chips and trinkets arranged neatly in rows. It didn't bring us any luck that evening, though, I remember. Cricket was afraid to dig sang, afraid that on the mountain we would be shot for rebels or runaways. We ran the Holsom Slough trotline and cleaned two puny catfish, who were probably glad to be collected after waiting on the line for three days. I told Cricket how downcast I had felt that morning watching Lee's soldiers, not expecting any sympathy, because he always did get on me for being too much of a "townie," but I got some: he told me to watch my back because "the only where white folks go from mean is meaner." I was inclined to agree, or at least to worry about it, for there I was stuck there in the middle of it all, with only my mama and myself amidst hordes of whites who were becoming less restrained in their viciousness every day. From old Deihl, a Yank and an abolitionist in his way (though surely Brown had redefined that term), I felt no danger but no protection either. I had never particularly envied Cricket the "idiocy of rural life," as Marx calls it, but I did sometimes envy him living among his own people. The ignorance and superstition of the plantation slaves, which usually annoyed or disgusted me, seemed almost like a charm as I sat among them that night, welcomed simply because I was who I was. African. And if I wanted a show of martial strength, there it was: the fire on the mountain, burning as steadily as a star, bringing comfort to its friends and terror to its enemies. Indeed, the fire on the mountain was to turn out, in the long run, more effective than any of Lee's parades. But the long run can be a long time running.

September 26
Miss Laura Sue Hunter
Mint Springs
Staunton, Virginia

Dear Lee Little Laura Sue:

Don't believe everything you hear. I was at exams, not at Bethel Church, though I had friends there who did indeed hear Douglass: who is hardly the Devil Incarnate as our father would have it, but only seeking that which God ordains, indeed, commands, all men to seek. Nor did he call for the blood of all Whites. Don't listen to our father, or any slave owner, for that matter, on political matters.

I found your young Bewley's poem very nice, though I am less given than he to regular meter. I do hope that in addition to Honor and Courage, he will consider Sentiment among Man's estate. I look forward eagerly to meeting him in Baltimore next week, and to seeing you also. I must tell you, Lee Little Sister, in all confidence, that I, also, have met Someone, a woman (not *merely* a Lady) I have known for a while but only recently discovered in my own heart the feelings which I have not yet disclosed to her. She is from the North. I will tell all when I see you next week. Meanwhile, not a word!

On his return Payson will be passing through Staunton with my bay, Emmanuel, which was street-injured and doesn't take to Philadelphia. Please remind our father to ask old Hosea to check his withers; he was always the best with horses. I can find no vet here who has the way with animals of our Virginia Colored.

> Your Loving and Intrigued Brother,
> Thomas

Grissom had been a revolutionary for forty-seven years: in wars for twenty-one, six of these overseas (he was a veteran of Berlin as well as Chicago); in prison for eleven; in peace for nine. Peace had its own difficulties. Yasmin was right. Old Mrs. Hunter was an unreconstructed racist (no surprise), and he was an opportunist for catering to her so uncritically. He could find a way to relate to the old folks in the area without accommodating himself so completely to their political backwardness. He would write to Yasmin, accept her criticism, and thank her for it. The incident had made saying good-bye a little awkward when he dropped her at Cardwell's. She was in a hurry to get to Staunton. It was odd how childishly she dealt with her husband's death. How easy it is to spot other people's weaknesses!

Grissom hoped she got onto the highway before it started pouring rain. He punched on the radio and found the weather, but it sounded backward; it said the storm was finally breaking. But he could see the top of the Blue Ridge, even now, gathering clouds around it like a cloak . . . Then he realized that the weather report was not about the Shenandoah at all, but about Mars. Faraway Mars. The weather had broken and the ship was going down. Grissom would have sat in the car to hear the rest, but when he pulled into his garage in back of the museum the phone was ringing—the high-pitched, close-together rings that meant the caller was holding the "urgent" button all the way down. Not bothering with his crutches for the first time in years (and amazed at how fast he could move without them), Grissom got through the door and caught it.

It was Yasmin.

"Harriet is gone," she said.

☆ ☆ ☆

Lee moved fast, and then he moved slow. Within a week of Quarry Road, he had filled the Valley with troops; then for another week he marched them around in circles. They arrived all at once on trains on the newly repaired track from north, south, and east (there were neither tracks nor roads through the blue wall of the Cumberlands to the west). The population of the town doubled, all with men, all of them white, most of them young and filled with a festive spirit. They were going slave-hunting. There was artillery in light blue uniform from Connecticut and Ohio, for this was before the abolitionists began their work in the ranks; the Richmond Grays with their beaver hats, and North Carolina militia too; trainloads of cadets, who looked naked to me now without the black flies on their throats, though this time they would not walk point up the mountain. There was cavalry as well; and even with their own provender and smiths and spares there was profit for old Deihl, whose face showed those seams that passed for smiles in those days. Having filled Charles Town with troops, having stirred it with the steel spoon of martial ceremony, Lee let it simmer for a week. There were balls with the local debutantes (such as they were) for the billeted officers (such as they were); turkey shoots for the enlisted men; bowling on the green; horseshoes; horse races; and, new to our backward, over-the-mountain area, duels. These were not blood fights but half-load, triple-waistcoat Virginia gentleman duels—but what did we know? At first they caused quite a stir among the town boys, among whom I still included myself for such adventures as these. Three times at dawn that week there were shots on the sycamore flats near Caney Creek, and all three times the brush piles were filled with boys' expectant eyes. What disappointment—a bar fight was bloodier than these affairs! Every morning there was drilling in the town square, and every afternoon on the outskirts, more drilling, near the Charles Town racetrack, where the bulk of the troops were tented. Lee made no secret of his plans. He was to trap Brown and Tubman on the mountain between the deep gap where the rivers plunged through, at Harper's Ferry, and Key's Gap, a high notch some eight miles to the south, past Iron Bridge. Lee's second-in-command was J.E.B. Stuart, the same who was later to become infamous in the campaign of southwestern Virginia; he controlled the Loudon Valley to the east of the Blue Ridge with a smaller force. As the Federals saw it, the heavily populated eastern valleys were less hospitable to Brown even though there were more black people there, because they were slaves and afraid of the "abs"—unlike the free blacks of the Harper's Ferry area, whom Lee suspected of supporting Brown. This illusion (that slaves fear freedom) cost Lee plenty; it cost him the Shenandoah Valley campaign; it cost him, in fact, Brown. Harper's Ferry was easy enough to secure. The south side of the Potomac for two miles was blue with troops, though these were not Lee's best, for no one thought that Brown would break that way. Meanwhile, mounted pickets covered Key's Gap, up the hill from Iron Bridge, seasoned men with the new Henry repeaters. Brown was trapped, and Lee was playing with him. I watched all these preparations with the dumb fascination of a turkey on the stump watching the ax get fetched; that was, I think, the point of them. Looking back, I can see that Lee's assault was as much on the sensibilities of the Africans watching and waiting as on the actual few (so far) who had picked up arms. And, of course, it was all designed to succor and reassure the whites, abolitionists as well as slavery supporters, since all (or most) were making it clear in the newspapers of the North that as much as they hated slavery (oh, none could hate it more!), they abhorred murder and insurrection worse. The whites were closing ranks while we were yet to do this. Colonel Lee was in no hurry. He had his Captain Brown and he was playing with him. I heard his strategy discussed with perfect candor at Mama's table by cavalry sergeants and mule-skinners alike. Moving with vastly superior numbers, from east and west at once, while the gaps to the north and south were sealed, in high daylight, after a devastating cannonade, Lee intended to squeeze Brown onto the narrow mountaintop and swat him and his pitiful hundred men like a single fly. Lee's expedition numbered 2,600 in all, of whom 900 were to ascend the Blue Ridge. It was not to be a battle; this was, in their eyes, extermination, not war. It was not a fox hunt but a mad-dog clubbing. There were no provisions to bring prisoners down. It was assumed by now that the renegade whites would not give up; and the blacks, after such an escapade, were valueless. It was over for them all. The town had a week to consider all this. Pity and scorn for Brown's fanatical enthusiasm was balanced with admiration for Lee's deliberation, regularity, determination, and strength. For six days we were all awaiting this great execution while Lee drilled his men and moved his artillery into place on the Bolivar Heights at the foot of the ridge. But except for the morning duels of the hungover officers (which we boys now slept through), not a shot was fired. On Friday, September 29, the Washington train brought across the newly repaired Maryland bridge a great rifled gun the size of a church steeple, riding on a flat car and covered with soldiers, newspapermen, excursionists, and boys looking for excitement; they had ridden the train all the way from Frederick, Maryland—some from Washington! The giant Ericsson gun (named after its Swedish inventor, who was along in a club car, with his own entourage) was parked on a siding near the stockyard, then moved because of the smell to the Fairgrounds on the east side of Charles Town. Clearly the plan was not only to punish Brown but punish the mountain as well for sheltering him; to knock it down. On Sunday night I stole out to Green Gables. The fire on the mountain no longer looked brave, but stupid, like the fevered eye of an idiot; like the eye of the turkey watching the ax get fetched. I wished it weren't even there. I wished they had run away, but of course it was too late for that; there was no place to go. Since Little John, no one was slipping up the mountain; it would have made about as much sense as hiding in the muzzle of the Ericsson gun. Cricket said old man Calhoun still hadn't reported Little John's loss: not only was there uncertainty about the insurance claim, but there were rumors that owners of rebel slaves would be assessed for the damages caused by Brown, and perhaps even for the expense of Lee's expedition. These rumors all, of course, turned out to be groundless. On Monday morning, October 1, at precisely 7:00 A.M., the cannonade began with the Ericsson gun firing from the siding near the Fairgrounds. I was in the barn helping Deihl with the horses, and the great boom shivered the water in my pail. It sounded like a giant door slamming shut in the sky. It was echoed by the smaller pieces at the foot of the mountain; then a distant rumble from over the mountain in the Loudon Valley. There was no more work that morning. The battle was joined.

There were signs of war everywhere, but not of humankind's puny conflicts; the giant stones had been piled up not by Lee's cannonade of a hundred years before, but by the slow vast collision of the continents a hundred million years before that. The mountainside discouraged thought. There was no view, no turns in the path—just a long, straight, steady tramp leading up the slope, inviting neither hurry nor rest. That was all right. Harriet didn't feel like thinking, hurrying, or resting. She felt like walking.

She had worried about the new shoes, but the walk seemed to loosen them up. They seemed almost to glow with it.

The timber was thick, and the trail wound around and through giant boulders, following a slash that had been made by loggers snaking tulip poplars down 150 years before. It was not Brown's actual trail—or was it? This land had already been lived in and timbered over a hundred years when the war began—or had it? Harriet wished Grissom were along to explain such things, but the trail was not for a one-legged man. She couldn't believe her mother had looked at her crossed-eyed for asking him about hiking. She could tell it made him feel bad, but so what? Sometimes missing things was the next best thing to having them.

She picked up a rock and carried it for twenty steps, curious to know what it was like to haul a ten-pound Sharps rifle up a hill; but a rock had no place to hold on to. Harriet dropped it and stopped to rest. It was probably easier if somebody was shooting at you from behind. She was glad her mother was having a baby. Who wouldn't be?

She looked at the map Grissom had given her. Her mother would be getting back soon and finding her gone, but the mountain was bigger than it looked on the map.

Well, let her worry a little. What were mothers for?

Meanwhile, great plops fell on the map.

For one thing, it was starting to rain.

☆ ☆ ☆

Even Mama quit what she was doing. She walked out into the yard and watched the cannonade, her face a blank, still wearing her apron while the biscuits hardened in the oven and the fire went out. Every six minutes exactly, the ground shook as the Ericsson gun went off a mile across town. By 7:25 they had found their range, and with every shot a puff of smoke would dance off the top of the ridge near the fire—which could be seen in the daylight from Charles Town for the first time. Or maybe it was just the first time I had noticed. It seemed bigger than ever. Unless the shells hit near the top of the ridge, we couldn't see them; in the deeper woods along the lower slopes, the shots disappeared like raindrops into grass. By noon the Charles Town–Harper's Ferry Road was filled with buggies filled with white folks, watching and picnicking, local and from as far away as Strasburg and Winchester. Mama, of course, had to use up the hard biscuits as ham biscuits, and sent me with the two girls, neither of whom I could tolerate, to sell them. All the rest of the black folks, including the kids my age, were watching from the fields and fence rows, and staying away from the road which was choked with white folks. I sold about half my biscuits and then found Cricket and two other Green Gables boys

near a brush arbor church at the edge of town, and we shared
the rest (I told Mama that two white boys had stolen them). At
noon the troops moved out, bugles and all, and at two, it was
announced, they moved up the mountain. Like the cannon hits,
the soldiers were invisible under the trees and in the trackless
laurel, now ragged (I imagined) with shot. I watched the whole
thing with cold fascination. It was like watching a whipping or
a hanging (or so I thought at the time, so I thought). I honestly
don't know to this day what the other Africans were thinking
while they watched, but I was thinking with the terrible smug
certainty of the true slave that Brown and Tubman and Little
John and the wounded soldier I had given Sees Her on the
Green Gables lawn, all deserved this whipping; that they were
fools for disregarding what every schoolboy knew: that the
power of the whites, once marshaled, was irresistible; what boy,
black or white, didn't know this? To ignore this law of nature
seemed the height of perversity. So I was as surprised as the
whites when Lee's men marched back at dusk unbloodied,
humiliated, empty-handed. I heard the story a hundred times
in the next week and a hundred more in the fifty years after,
and I have no doubt, great-grandson, you are hearing it still, in
1959, fifty years from now: They had gained the top of the ridge
and found only the fire—not a man, not a mule, not a gun, nary
a hat nor boot nor coat; no bodies, no blood, no nothing. Only
the fire was there, blazing out of the rock fortress known forever
afterward as False Fire, roaring as if someone had just thrown
a rick of wood on it. Brown and Tubman and their men had
slipped away like blackbirds. Like foxes. Like wild Indians.
Like smoke into the wind or fish into the sea. Like Africans. We
have had the same three hundred years to learn to hide our
smiles, that white folks have had to perfect their scowls. The
whole town turned stunned, nasty, cold like a December driz-
zle, even though it was not quite October; and I walked softly,

gingerly home, avoiding the streets. Lee waited for darkness to ride in that night on his great gray horse, certified a fool; and late that same night, that very same bold dark life-giving night, Brown and Tubman struck twice, from the east and from the south: burning a courthouse (at Black Creek) and for the first time a church. The big Ericsson gun was swabbed down and wheeled away (lest they steal it?). The fire reappeared on the mountain farther down the Valley, then on one ridge to the east. And Lee turned to terror.

☆ ☆ ☆

October 6, 1859
Miss Laura Sue Hunter
Miss Colby's School
Richmond

Dear Laura Sue:

No, upon my very life, I will not apologize for what you call my insult to your young man's Honor. Our Uncle Reuben has written on the same Subject and I would expect to hear from Father, were he in his health. Honor is sufficient unto itself; what I injured last week was not Bewley's Honor but his Pride. I called him a Pup only because he has not quite yet attained the full stature of a Dog. Gentlemen have the right (indeed, some would say, the obligation) to disagree. But no man, Southern or Northern, family or otherwise, calls Frederick Douglass, Negro though he be, such a name in my presence and walks away unchallenged.

Perhaps like so many others, young Bewley was unhinged by his Commander's recent humiliation at Harper's Ferry. So be it. I would remind him that Defeat demands more of a gentleman than Victory.

I only wish that you might prefer to marry a man rather than a provincial sycophant, which is what these days our poor South demands more and more of her beleaguered sons, as the clouds of War gather.

> Your ever faithful but
> never remorseful brother,
> Thomas &c.

☆ ☆ ☆

Many people date the formal beginning of the Independence War from Lee's Christmas defeat at Roanoke, because it marks the entry of Garibaldi and Mexico, Haiti and the Cherokee, Douglass's proclamation, and the internationalization of the conflict; but for myself and I suspect for many of the folk in the Valley, the war began at the end of September, with False Fire. War raged up and down the Shenandoah all that fall and winter. Lee struck at Brown, but it was like striking at smoke, and in frustration and rage (or so it seemed at the time, but as we found out later, the worst of his outrages were calculated), he struck at the people: the black people, of course. For every plantation torched, east and south (Brown's particular strategic genius was that there were none to the west or north), a freedman's cabin was torched or pulled down by oxen while the children watched and wailed. For every militia man or slave owner killed, or even injured, a woman or child was found murdered. Or sometimes both in one, as in the notorious incident of Katy Creek, which even the North heard about, where a pregnant woman was hanged by a "drunken" band of soldiers. At first Lee struck with his regulars, but they balked, and after the protests in Congress, where the Southerner had more enemies than the African had friends, Lee began to use his irregulars. They were often the same men out of uniform, or militiamen, or "Kentucks" from across the Cumberlands: the same bloodthirsty adventurers who had purloined Texas from Mexico only a few decades before (for the planters' pockets, not their own: but no one said, least of all myself, that these were not fools). Still landless, these roughians were still gathering land for the landed! I knew them well enough, since it was they, not the gentlemen, who took their cornbread and sweet potato pie with my mother, and left their ill-starred horses to my indifferent care. Every Wednesday there was a hanging in Charles Town, as regular as prayer meeting. It was usually a "sympathizer" of Brown and Tubman, since few members of their little army had yet been taken alive. It got to be a weekly ceremony of terror; the whites packed lunches, and even some black folks (God in His infinite depravity licensing every outrage) circulated through the crowd selling chicken wings. Meanwhile, Mama and Deihl were making plans to move North. Old Deihl had promised to move back to Pennsylvania and free her (and me) someday, and Brown and Lee conspired together to move that date ahead. Deihl was somewhat reluctant to leave, with the money rolling in. But all could see the gathering storm, and I suspect Mama talked some sense into the old man, which was a talent she had.

October 12, 1859
Miss Emily Pern
Queens Dispensary
Bath, England

Dear Emily:

I wait eagerly to hear from you. I do hope England suits you well. You must know that as some things inch Forward, others fly Backward, and I have now been challenged to the Ten Paces, by the very young man that my little sister wishes to marry. It seems that by only calling him a Pup instead of smacking him like one last week, as was my inclination, in Baltimore, on the occasion of an insult to my Ideals (I don't guard my honor so closely), I gravely wounded not only his Pride (at which I confess I had taken Aim) but his Family. He is this very morning in Philadelphia with two cousins—calling on me—and my father has sent an old family slave, by train, with two Longmann duelling pistols, too valuable to trust to the post, anxious that I don't let this chance pass to fire a salute to Feudalism. My family first asks me to apologize; and failing that, wishes me to shoot the man!

However, I will not so honor Barbarism and have refused to see my challenger. The irony is that my family is pressing this duel upon me, while it was a remark about their arch-Satan, Douglass, to which I took exception.

As to the political situation you left behind: Rumors are flying here since the recently poorly publicized but well-known failure of Lee's operation. The streets are filled with foreigners, and it is much rumored, agents, of this government, European governments, "interested parties," idealists, mercenaries, moral reformers, romantics, and adventurers of every stripe. There is talk of an international detachment of Garibaldini gathering in Mexico to aid the rebels, and, some say, recapture Texas and even California. Levasseur (who sends his compliments) just got back from New York where, he says, German Socialists, veterans of '48, are openly drilling with arms in Union Square. In St. Louis street fighting has erupted between the Socialists and the Know-Nothings and local Copperheads. Meanwhile, one of our Medical Group was called home with Connecticut's 125th Guard, which was ordered to the Shenandoah, mutinied (or, at least, refused), and offered up an abolitionist resolution in support of Captain John Brown! They are not likely to be hanged in Danbury. This was, my friend writes, in emulation of the Massassoit Guard, the Negro regiment of Concord and Boston (which is openly recruiting the free colored of the Bay State, and not, the Governor complains, to guard the Constitution.) What a wind of freedom is blowing through America today! I pity you, banished to stuffy old imperial England. There is talk of rebellion among the Molly Maguires in Pennsylvania, the Irish, even in America, eager to strike a blow at England through attacking the Slavery that feeds her dark satanic mills; for it is well known that the English are active among that element of southern Federalists (actually Monarchists with no King but Slavery) who talk of an independent slave-nation, as if such a soul-less Frankenstein's creature could walk, even supported by England on the one arm and New England on the other. The blacks of Canada, who come from both the U.S. and the Carib Sea, have raised a company in Chatham which they are openly equipping to land in the Carolinas, some say to hide their real intentions to infiltrate through the Ohio Valley. Many are from Cincinnati. What a wind! What a light burns atop that old Blue Ridge mountain, which beheld every scene of my youth! I wish I could see it myself. It seems to have stirred up everyone's deepest feelings and ambitions; God knows what hatreds have been awakened in the South. The struggle is spreading, as the South feared and old Brown hoped, beyond the Blue Ridge; several Tidewater estates have been burned (one belonging to a branch of my Family) and of course every depredation and piece of banditry is blamed on Brown and Tubman. Perhaps this is all to the good. Certainly there is no more debate about whether the Negro will fight for freedom. The question is, since Iron Bridge, moot. Now the question is, who will win? My own Opinion I must admit has gone through substantial alterations.

As for *your friend* here, I am well. Our work gathering medical materials is so far either unnoticed or unbothered by the authorities, but I am not so naive as not to expect an investigation or Grand Jury soon, not to mention a Copperhead attack.

And you? I would dearly like to hear from you. Though you are less than a month departed, I admit I miss your letters more than I would have thought. My emotions, like my opinions, have been in continual alteration here, putting all in a new light. How is Bath? And how is England? And how is School? And how is my dearly missed—friend—Emily?

Do please write.

Yours &c. &c.
Thos. (Hunter, M.D., *ad imminen*)

☆ ☆ ☆

"She would be back by now. Plus, there's nothing in the town she wanted to see. Plus, the center was closed this morning when we left, anyway. She doesn't even like museums; besides, you would have seen her there. She would have left a note. Ever since Leon . . . died, she's been super-considerate all the time; she babies me, really. Her own mother. Except when she's mad. She's been mad at me ever since I gave her those shoes. She has it in her head they don't look right. You know how kids are.

101

Or I don't know, maybe you don't. Shit, it's starting to rain.
There's something else; one thing I didn't tell you. Last night
I told her that I was pregnant."

"Oh," Grissom said.

His eyes dropped from Yasmin's broad face to her long figure. He would never have guessed. They were standing on the
steps of the Shenandoah Inn. He had come right over when she
called.

"Well, maybe that upset her," he said. "Maybe that's why
she didn't go with us to Martinsburg."

"She wasn't planning to go anyway," Yasmin said. "She said
she wasn't interested in some little old lady." She looked up and
laughed, and this time Grissom laughed with her.

"Maybe she went up the mountain," he said. "She was asking
me yesterday about the North Star Trail. Hey, I even gave her
a map."

Yasmin looked across the river. "Where does this trail
start?"

"Right there. It's nothing to worry about. These are little
bitty mountains."

"I don't see anything but bushes. She didn't seem upset last
night when I told her."

"How come you waited so long to tell her?"

"What do you mean?" Yasmin said, agitated again. "That's
not fair. When I picked her up in Staunton, it was the first time
I had seen her in four months."

"You waited a day and a night."

"You're right. I don't know."

"What did she say?"

"I don't remember. She didn't seem upset. Not about that,
anyway. You know what we talked about? Those damn shoes.
She doesn't think they look right, and you know what, at this
point I think she's right. I wish I had never gotten them. There's

something you're supposed to do to them, but I can't remember what it is. You know what else, Grissom? It suddenly just occurred to me."

"What?"

"She never asked me who the father was. Shit. Now look."

It was really starting to rain.

How well I remember the night that Mama sat me down at the board table in the kitchen and told me that she and Deihl were leaving Charles Town. Leaving Virginia. It was late October, cool enough so that the coal-burning cookstove, which in the summer urges children out the kitchen door, was drawing me toward it. The fire felt good. I stood first on one foot, then on the other. Old Deihl stood in the corner with his horse-smelling hat in his hand. Mama was the slave and he was the master, but she did all the talking and handled the money; they were that way. It was time to move North, Mama told me; troubles were coming to the Shenandoah. Deprivations, degradations, depredations, she said, using those Bible words that have been the solace of the ignorant and the learned alike for centuries. She mentioned neither Brown nor Tubman; never looked up and never looked east, toward the window and the mountain; but this was not peculiar to her, it was common to all the black folk in town, free and slave alike. Brown was like a woman's curse, accounted for by all but acknowledged by none, at least among ourselves. The plantation Africans were different, which is why lately I felt easier in their rough company, and often went to Green Gables to see the Fire on the Mountain. You could see it almost as well from town, but nobody looked. If Deihl could sell the stable, Mama said, we could be in "Balmer" (as folks called it then, great-grandson, and still do today) in a week.

Then on to Pennsylvania. There was plenty of money to be made up North (here old Deihl sucked his pipe like January wind in a chimney). It was too uncertain here in Virginia; there would be fighting and fires; there would be reprisals against black folks and their friends and families (Deihl again sucked his pipe); there would be famine and pestilence. Mama went on, describing poor little Charles Town and Harper's Ferry as if they were Sodom and Gomorrah, but I was hardly listening by then. I had one eye on the door, for I had to get to Green Gables and find Cricket. I wasn't concerned about moving North in a week, since I had already laid my plans: to meet with Cricket and join Brown and Tubman's Army that very night!

☆ ☆ ☆

October 20, 1859
Miss Emily Pern
Queens Dispensary
Bath, England

My Dear Emily:

I hope this reaches you in good health and Spirits. I passed my tutorial (hoorah!) and am preparing to go South after Thanks Giving, to take up practice. I am of course apprehensive. In fact, and I tell you only because this letter is entrusted to my friend Levasseur, who is on his way to England—I again recommend him to your affection and trust—in fact, I go on behalf of our Medical Assistance group to render aid to the rebel army there. The bold talk is done and the hour is gathering.

Ironically, the first victim of my plan to go back South is my principle against duelling. I wrote you that my sister's beau was seeking to challenge me; well, in order to preserve my image as a Virginia gentleman, essential for our success, I have agreed to meet him at dawn tomorrow on the Schuylkill. Duelling is of course illegal here, but any school with as many Southerners as Temple must have informal arrangements, and so there is a field where shots heard are not remarked. It is now midnight and I sit with two Longmann cap and ball pistols before me on the table where my texts have sat this past four years. What a blunt field of study is Death! I have loaded the guns with powder and wad but no shot, but we draw lots and his weapons, I suspect, will not be so solicitous of the Flesh. At any rate, it is not the violence of death I fear but its precipitous finality: that I might depart this world never having thanked those Parents who gave me life; or those friends who have given birth to my Spirit, such as yourself and my Jacobin, Lev. But Emily, let me be bold. You may have suspected that I harbor in my breast feelings, for you, that are somewhat more tender than I have expressed, thus far. Is it too much to hope that your inclinations, toward me, might also grow if encouraged? I would ask leave, when this evil work is done, to offer you a declaration, beyond this timid confession, that I hope will not surprise, or repel you. But enough said can be too much. So, for the present, I remain:

Your humble and Ob'd'n't servant, & admiring & affectionate friend. And, God willing, someday, perhaps more:

Thos. Hunter, M.D.
Tom

☆ ☆ ☆

For weeks, since False Fire, I had been plaguing Cricket to run away with me and join Brown's men. At first he had laughed scornfully; then he chided me that such talk was foolish, then dangerous. Only gradually did I begin to suspect, then understand, that there was more to his hesitancy than his usual obstinacy (that it was cowardice I had never believed); and that he himself was in contact with the Army of the North Star. I later found out, as we all did, the hard way, that he was in fact one of those who helped people and supplies find their way up the mountain (for they were back on the Blue Ridge, as well as on the mountains to the south) and perhaps helped the wounded find their way down. All this and more Cricket kept a secret as he kept everything else, by carrying it loose and open in his hand, by acting loose-lipped and foolish; he was perhaps the only African in the Valley who spoke openly and even admiringly about Brown, as though to be looting arsenals and burning courthouses were as admirable and thrifty as thinning trees. All this, I see now, was to remove him from suspicion as one of their confederates; it was Cricket's variation of the ancient deception we all played, one way or another, on the whites. The old folks played it by acting as if Brown were only more white folks' foolishness and contrary to all sense and understanding. Mama did it by acting as if freedom was the curse. I did it. Since Lee's defeat the fire was back on the mountain, but sporadically, shifting. Cricket's job was to bring the new recruits to the foot of the Blue Ridge, along the last section of the underground railway: the new section of track that had been laid by Brown and Tubman so that it no longer led North, to escape, but up the ridge and then South, to liberation. All this was told me later, or I figured it out, although who recruited Cricket and how, I was never told and I never asked. Even today, even after all these years, and the winning of independence and the building of socialism, I would not want to know, so dear to our Nova Africa is that deep silence of the slave: it is our liberty bell. But I knew none of this then. All I knew was that Brown and Tubman had outwitted Lee, and like a million other Africans who had been "waiting to see," I wanted to join them. Oh, Brown was our lion and Tubman our fox, great-grandson! If you won't go with me, I'll go by myself, I threatened Cricket; and with this he finally listened (we were putting bottle glass on his baby brother's grave) and stood up and cuffed me more tenderly than usual (as I see it now, through eyes washed clean by time and tears)— then looked me up and down, figuring, I guess, that there was only one way to shut me up. "Bring a piece of bread, a candle, a clasp knife and Deihl's pistol to Solomon's Pond tomorrow night," he told me. But Deihl doesn't have a pistol, I complained. He swatted me again and asked me if Deihl was a white man. I said, of course. Every white man has a pistol, fool, Cricket said. It's only a question of finding it. Sure enough, I found it later that night, the very same night that Mama told me we were moving North. It was an ancient Bavarian cap and ball with an octagon barrel, wrapped in a calico rag in a chest at the foot of the bed in the old man's upstairs room where he hardly ever stayed. It was as heavy as a coal stove, but stealing it was the easiest part. The hardest part was the note. Even though I knew she couldn't read it, I wrote Mama that I was gone to either Death or Glory, to fight and die for Freedom's flag. Then I wondered, who would read it to her, since few black folks who could read could be trusted (except of course myself). Also, Cricket had told me to follow his instructions exactly and leave *no clues.* So I tore the note up. Then, knowing I would never return, and Cricket would never know, I wrote it again and left it in Mama's oven, where Deihl would never look. By now it was time and my heart was pounding as I wrapped up a chunk of cheese and stole out of the house, out of the town, and down to the slough west of Charles Town and south of Harper's Ferry that was called Solomon's Pond. But the joke was on me: it was only a test. Cricket rebuked me for bringing the cheese (even as he ate it), saying that I must follow directions *precisely.* He told me to put the gun back where I'd found it and meet him exactly one week later at midnight at the abandoned firehouse at the edge of Charles Town, bringing absolutely nothing. Not even the gun? He laughed and said Brown had no need for antiques. He asked if I had written Mama a note. No, I lied. Cricket seemed pleased; he said good, don't bother, since we wouldn't be joining the rebels anyway but helping them from here in town. I was furious and disappointed, but before I could protest he was gone. I ran home and tore up the note and crept into bed long before sunrise.

October 22, 1859
Miss Emily Pern
Queens Dispensary
Bath, England

Dear Emily:

Well, yesterday I fought my first and hopefully final, Duel. I aimed to miss, but my opponent didn't; but he is a poor shot, which was gratifying, as we used his weapons from the toss instead of mine, which are falsely loaded with powder but no shot. We shook hands and though the incident is not forgotten, the episode is ended. Meanwhile he is off to join Lee's Army! Perhaps he will miss Brown. I felt the shot go by, which is like someone tearing up a letter close by your ear. A letter from Death you will have to read sooner or later. Speaking of letters, have you heard yet from our friend

Levasseur, now in London I think, who has sworn to
write me of England and of you? Tell him to write me
if you do. In short, I live, and hope to hear from you.

Your faithful &c.
Thomas

Harriet stepped up her pace, hoping to reach the top of the
mountain before it got too wet. She wished she had brought a
raincoat or something to eat. The first part of the walk had been
neat, through the laurel-covered ledges, but now it was just a
trudge. She couldn't find the right pace between fast and slow.
The shoes looked better, though. They had acquired a sort of
blue glow. Last night she'd had what her father and granny
called a "conjure dream": a dream where nobody in the dream
knew it was a dream but you. She was running down a dirt road;
the grown-ups were in front of her, walking fast, talking among
themselves and ignoring the kids, as grown-ups do. The kids
were behind her, going slow, pitching rocks, swatting weeds
with sticks. She was in the middle, alone, not sure whether she
wanted to catch up with the grown-ups or fall back with the
kids.

Then there was another kid with her in the middle, a boy she
didn't know. Even in the dream she knew it was her new
brother. Mama, she cried out, she wanted to show her mother,
but her mother was walking across the field away from the road
in her high blue Africa shoes, walking fast.

Now it was really starting to rain. What happened to living
shoes if you got them wet?

Maybe they turned into blue fish.

There was a hole in the rock, a dry ledge with a dirt floor,
like a little house, and Harriet climbed into it.

☆ ☆ ☆

If Cricket hadn't been so much bigger than me, I swear I would have hit him. I was frustrated and angry all week that I had been fooled. I didn't want to stay in town. I wanted to join Brown and Tubman and be a soldier; I was almost thirteen. But he wouldn't even talk about it. I know now all the arguments he could have made, but Cricket wasn't the arguing kind. He just told me to shut up and do what I was told. On the appointed night of our next meeting, I went to bed early, then lay awake until I could hear Mama's snore, and then Deihl's, like an old gospel duet, only she was the bass and he was the tenor. He sometimes went to her bed but not exactly as master and slave; there was a rough equality of affection between them because he had bought her promising to set her free. They had become man and wife in their way, but I was not included in the family. My own father had escaped right after Mama was bought (from Green Gables, where she was raised) and before I was born; and though I often wondered about him, she let me know that I was never to ask. When I thought of him, it was not of a man but of a wild goose heading north against the sky. The moon was setting at midnight when I crept out the back door, and I was surprised to find Cricket waiting for me by the woodpile, not at the assigned place. I was beginning to see that surprise was central to his method. Motioning to me, he started toward the barn. Suddenly I was afraid. I thought he was going to steal the horses. Slitting throats I could handle: war, arson, revolution—even murder—were fine with me. But stealing horses was going too far. I froze in my tracks, terrified, a living illustration of Marx's insight that our livelihood conditions our consciousness. Hissing like a snake, Cricket said *come on!* More afraid of him, I followed; but I needn't have worried. After patting the horses on the rump to calm them, Cricket took the hurricane lamp from the wall, explaining later on the road that

110

the one he had planned to bring from Green Gables had broken that day in a kitchen accident. My job was to keep my mouth shut and follow him like a shadow and do what he told me. Period. We stopped at a little church on Westall's Road, where Cricket pulled a gun wrapped in a rag out from under the side steps, and stuck it in his belt. This was no antique, but a sleek little LeFebre four-shot revolver. Then he pulled out two black cloths and tied one onto his face and one onto mine, like highwaymen. Then we were back on the road. We made for the fence row once when we heard horses: a team of six paddy rollers rode by, making enough noise for an army. Times being what they were, they were not wanting to take anybody by surprise. After an hour of walking, we got to Buford Hollow Church. Cricket cooed like a dove from the shadows, and we both stood hidden in the deep womanly darkness of a willow tree, shoulder to shoulder like babies in the womb. He cooed again. There was a coo back, and from behind the outhouse came a dark shape as black as the night that enfolded us, carrying a shotgun. "Liberty," Cricket whispered, and only when the other croaked back, "Death," did I realize it was a woman, not a man—an older woman about Mama's age, forty-five. She looked hungry and worried. Cricket handed her the bread, and took her gun and handed it to me. She was reluctant to give it up. It was a beautifully tooled English shotgun, some slave-owning family's heirloom. Even in the darkness the silver locks gleamed. Cricket told the woman to turn around and tied a mask across her face like ours. Then, while she waited, he filled his palm with small gravel and poured it down the barrel of the gun, then tamped it with a piece of biscuit using a willow wand as ramrod, and handed it back to me. "Insurance," he told me later; and we were off. No talk, no names. My heart was pounding, but I said nothing, only played the shadow. I covered the silver lock of the gun with my hand because I felt it gleamed like a beacon. After another hour on the road, we reached a forest, and Cricket plunged into the pitch-black woods, the woman following Cricket; and me, her. We came out in an open space which, even in the darkness, I could sense was a quarry. We walked to the middle on a jumble of great rocks. There we sat until Cricket saw or heard some sign that I missed, and lighted the hurricane lamp, setting it at his feet turned very low. We sat longer until a light flashed in the woods; then at Cricket's gesture I handed him the shotgun and he handed it to the woman, and we were gone without a word, taking the now-extinguished lamp and leaving her alone in the darkness. Now it was I who was sorry to give up the gun. On the road back we took off the masks. We got home right before dawn, and I replaced the lamp in the barn and slipped into my bed above the kitchen. Two hours later I was up doing my kitchen chores; then it was to the barn, where I did my stable chores; then to the house to help serve dinner. I wasn't tired; I was in heaven. I kept playing it over and over in my mind: the darkness, the cool machinery of the heavy guns, the whispers and the cooing signals. The mysteriousness of war. We were the shadows the fire on the mountain cast. Shoulder to shoulder with Cricket in the dark, I had found what I was looking for. Thus ended my first trip. Alas, there was to be only one more.

October 18
Laura Sue Hunter
Mint Springs Farm
Staunton, Virginia

Dear Laura Sue:

I am glad to hear the news, but I ask you, what does it mean that your brother's taking a shot at your beau is the occasion for your marrying him? How far we have come from the Southern Ideal, in which, I seem to recall, the women tearfully tried to restrain the men from their Duels, instead of rewarding them? Or perhaps I had it backward. Seriously, little sister, please accept my Congratulations, and my apologies for all that was said before. My compliments, also, to my future brother-in-law and former Adversary. With luck, I will be home by Thanks Giving. How is Father? I fear the worst.

Your Loving Brother,
Thomas *(Targetus)*

☆ ☆ ☆

Our second trip was a week later, and started like the first. I met Cricket at the firehouse at midnight, and we picked up the lantern, and two miles down the road, at the little whitewashed Westall's Road church, crouching under the steps, the revolver. Cricket waited until then to put the mask on my face and warn me again to say absolutely nothing. This time our contact waited in the bushes near the ford of Greasy Creek, not waiting for the cooing dove but coming out of the bushes eagerly. "Liberty," he said, getting (I think) the password backward; this time it was Cricket who answered, "Death." He was a man of about thirty, a stooped, mournful slave disfigured from a whipping who I had seen around Charles Town on Sundays. "Hey, sport," he said, reaching for the side of my head as if to scratch it, as men do to boys when no dogs are around; but Cricket slapped his hand. The slap was startlingly loud and must have stung. No words, Cricket said, with no words. The man had a gun that Cricket reached for and handed to me. This was no English fowling piece. It was a loose old trade musket, the stock split and held together with wire. But it had a cap fitted, so I guessed it was loaded. Again Cricket poured small stones down the barrel and tamped them with a biscuit before trusting me with it. Insurance again—not only that the gun was loaded, but that I couldn't miss anything at close range. Things were a little grim after the slap, and we paraded through the night in single file, in perfect silence, Cricket in front, the man in the middle, and I at their back with the shotgun. The moon sank behind the Cumberlands far to the west, and the valley put on the darkness like its own black mask. We kept to the road with one eye on the fence rows. The only place we were in danger of getting caught out was at Iron Bridge, across the Shenandoah, where if the paddy rollers came we would have no place to hide: bad for both them and us, since I had resolved to kill at least one slaver before I traded this soldiering for death; but we were across and in the dark wood-shaded road on the other side in less than a minute. We were taking a different route to the same quarry, I guessed. At a steep cut, Cricket swung up off the road into the laurel on an invisible trail. Our "traveler" hesitated; "Go on," I said before remembering I wasn't supposed to talk. The two of us were alone. The older man turned and looked at me, then grinned and followed Cricket. Unlike the woman the night before, he was careful not to snap the branches back in my face. I wished Cricket hadn't been so hot-blooded and slapped him. We ended up in the same quarry, entering from a different side: I could tell, even though this time it was pitch black. We picked our way across and around huge boulders with square edges, white and ghostly; I could make out their shapes, even though we couldn't see them; and sat down on a flat rock somewhere near the center of the space. I was all ears, curious to discover what signal Cricket was waiting for before lighting his light. We sat silently. Cricket broke a dry biscuit and handed us both a piece. The "traveler" fumbled in his pocket and I smelled tobacco. He struck a match and Cricket just as suddenly struck it out of his hand, whispering, "Fool." In one of those inexplicable acts of prescience by which our individual destinies are shaped, I pulled back the lock of the gun. It was quiet again. I ate my biscuit. Then suddenly we were jumped from behind. I heard Cricket groan and go down hard. I twisted away from a claw that held my shoulder and smelled the sharp unwashed smell of white men as I rolled backward off the rock, my feet reaching for the sky. The gun went off, I don't know how—I had neither the presence of mind nor the control to fire it—and there was a scream. There was another shot. My feet found dirt and I lit out running. Somehow I found the woods, or perhaps I should say they found me, taking me into their dark enfolding arms as a woman takes up a terrified child, while behind me a white man screamed, "My eye, my God, I'm shot, my eye, my God, my eye!" Another voice screamed, "Shut him up, by God!" All this screaming about God made me realize my own eyes were shut; I opened them, but I couldn't see; yet I knew perfectly where to go. I slipped like a shadow between two rotten logs and lay breathing, listening desperately for Cricket's footsteps behind me, in front of me, or at least his voice somewhere; but I heard nothing. I thought then they had cracked his skull. I heard our "traveler" say: There was a little one, there was a little one! And I knew—I had already known it—that he had betrayed us. The white man was still screaming. Shut him up, another said. "Shoot him?" another asked. "No, God d—— it, just shut him up." I don't know what they did, but there was silence. Then, startlingly, there was another shot and a voice yelled, "What? Are you shot? God d——, he shot the other 'nigger'!" "I thought he was out." "Don't kill him, don't kill him." Chillingly, I heard Cricket groan again. Then the others talked more calmly, "Let me tie this 'nigger' up and get Will to the doctor." . . . "Help me drag him." . . . "Where's Harrison with that God d—— mule?" . . . "Help me tie this 'nigger' on that mule." "Forget him, the back of his head is gone." Gone. I knew then that they had killed Cricket, and while they were still making noise I slipped away, leaving the gun which I had no way to reload, to rot forever under the logs. It was six miles to Charles Town, and I was all the way in the fence rows. I arrived at dawn with my arms slashed and bleeding from the blackberry bushes. I was amazingly calm and clear-minded, as if I had just awakened from a dream. My mind was as empty as a turned-over wash basin; it rang like tin. I knew the betrayer had known me and would be coming to get me, but it never occurred to me to run, not with Cricket dead. All I could think of was to sell my life dear. I re-stole Deihl's old horse pistol, primed it, cocked it, loaded it with "insurance," and climbed with it into the corner of the hayloft just as the sun was coming up. There I must have fallen asleep. I woke up hearing boys shouting in the street. It was afternoon. They were bringing Cricket into town on a wagon in chains, while boys raced after him, shouting he was going to hang, hang, hang. It wasn't Cricket who was dead but our "traveler," our betrayer, whom he had shot. Thus he had saved my life. Luckily Deihl was down the Valley, and it was Mama who found me in the barn and put me behind the stove in the kitchen, where I slept all night, she said, tossing and muttering in what the old Africans call "conjure dreams," in which your dreaming self is awake. In the dreams Cricket was dead again, and John Brown was an old woman, like a granny woman, an African; and she carried him through the door of the house, over and over, as they do when a woman dies in childbirth, to free the baby's spirit so she can't keep him with her in death, for the dead are jealous. But Cricket wouldn't wake up. Wouldn't wake up. Wouldn't wake up.

It had quit raining by the time Yasmin neared the top of the ridge. The wind was blowing the clouds away like leaves, and the leaves away like clouds. Now there was almost a view, but she wasn't interested. Where was that child? She was glad she had come ahead. Grissom had quit trying to talk her out of climbing the mountain once she had convinced him that (a) walking was good for pregnancy and (b) it was her daughter up there, so she was determined to go. He had given her two raincoats and a map, dropped her halfway up the mountain where a road crossed the trail, then driven in her car to Bear Pond Gap to wait, so they could drive down instead of walking.

Yasmin felt like a Jewish mother on a vid comedy, chasing her daughter with a raincoat through the rain. The odd thing was, she liked it. Her legs felt strong, and the fire in her belly seemed to warm her, float her over the stones rather than slow her down, as she'd thought it might (without telling Grissom). As she neared the top of the ridge, she could make out the valley below, looking scrubbed in the new sunlight peeping out between the clouds and the Cumberlands far to the west. Only an hour or two of daylight was left. Was she going to get stuck up here in the dark?

She should have called Staunton.

Where was that child?

The trail wound through a little nest of rocks before leveling out at what looked like the top, and Yasmin, no lover of nature, wondered: what if there's a bear? She went ahead. It wasn't a bear she heard, but a sound as ancient and elemental.

She heard a child crying.

I think the hardest lesson I ever learned was that war was not, nor was it ever meant to be, nor could it be bent to be, the answer to a boy's prayer. I learned this when they hung Cricket on Sunday afternoon, October 23, 1859, at 1:00 P.M. By noon the square was filled with white folks. They do love a hanging.

117

Not just the Kentuck and Tennessee roughnecks I knew every day from Mama's (and if they only knew it, probably from the quarry as well), but the little old churchgoing ladies, their baskets filled with beaten biscuits and chicken wings, their whiskers floured with disappearing powder; and the children, the white boys my age: all of my rivals and allies from those long-ago times when we spent afternoons chucking rocks at toads set loose on shingles on the river: as long ago as Adam and Eve, and *sic transit terror,* the toads at least were thankful. They were exactly one half hour off on the time. At half past noon the marshals brought Cricket out from the back of the jail. They mostly dragged him; he couldn't walk. Mama found out later when we buried him they had cut off his toes and botched it; had done it clumsily, poorly, incompletely, like everything those despicable sorry crackers did. With a dull ax. His face was swollen and his eyes were almost swollen shut. His hands were tied behind his back over a short pole so that he looked at first as if he were going to be crucified. I hardly recognized him. Perversely, I was glad. I was afraid he would see me and signal me to help him, and then what would I do? We had a hundred signals but none for this. But Cricket made it much easier than that for me. He looked like a sleepwalker, oblivious to the whole ceremony. In fact, I think the hard part was over, for him, and the hanging was a welcome end. Lee's bailiff read an order, and there was a smooth drum roll (they always managed that well), and the crowd hushed and surged forward, although many on the street still passed by on their normal everyday business. This was, after all, the Shenandoah in late 1859 and hanging a "nigger" was hardly an occasion. There was a wide gallows on the square, left up from last week when a man and his wife and her father had all swung together. The hangmen were all white. They wouldn't use black hangmen until later in the war. I was so confused and agitated that I searched the crowd in vain for

118

the black Judas that had betrayed us, then remembered that I was alive because he was dead; that the shot I thought had killed Cricket had killed him; and that Cricket had shot him and saved my life, because he knew me. I forced myself to look at Cricket's battered face and grew very conscious of the scratches on my face and arms from my flight through the fence rows. In terror (again) I backed up and looked all around me, but white folks never notice anything about us except our attitude toward them. Understand, great-grandson, at this point I was not myself (or perhaps I was): I was at the same moment angry, scared, vengeful, and even confident: like a church organ some madman was playing, with every stop open and every pipe surging with a different emotion, all unknown and new. How many must ever watch a brother hang? (For I was to find out later that very day that Cricket was not my cousin but my brother.) Mixed with my terror was hope, from my conjure dream. I knew Brown had a plan, else why the dream? The weed of hope grows wild in the soil of desperation. I wanted to catch Cricket's eye and tell him not to give up, that Brown and Tubman would never let him die, but I was too far back in the crowd. I had been backing away and now I could barely see him. I slipped forward through the crowd, making myself small, as kids can still do at twelve, until I was at the front, by the scaffold. Too close now. Cricket's eyes were blank like a dead man's. He stared off toward the Blue Ridge, where there was no fire that day, and seemed to feel and hear nothing. Two white man held his stick while a third bent down and tied his feet. It looked like a scene from the Bible, and I have never wondered since why those bloodthirsty crackers loved that book so well, that encyclopedia of torments; it is their favorite story. I moved back into the crowd, now afraid Cricket would see me, point at me, call like a dove, give me away. My blood was pounding: fear, hate, love. I was listening for that sweet

119

rolling thunder of horses, like the night at Green Gables. I was waiting for the crack of Sharps carbines. I scanned the rooftops where Lee's marines stood looking down, bored, never suspecting that in a second, or maybe two, black hands would cover their faces while knives opened their throats like books for the sky to read. Oh, did I yearn for that blood! I heard a whicker and a creak of harness behind me, and I turned, almost expecting to see that African warrior I had mounted on Sees Her, his face a storm of righteousness, his Sharps like held lightning . . . but it was only old Isaac the milk horse who had heard, I now believe, the Angel of Death fly over. Those dry wings. I turned back and my dreams were gone. The crowd was gasping, thrilled, and they were hanging Cricket. I would have screamed, but there was no scream in my throat to scream; like Cricket, I couldn't breathe. I ran backward, my arms flapping at my eyes, sucking for air, then hit a Kentuck's bony knee and fell sprawling. He bent down and lifted me up, but not as a man lifts a fallen child. No: grinning. As easily as if I were a four-year-old, he lofted me high over his shoulder, saying to his friends: Let's give this little "nigger" a better look. Another took my feet and they pushed me forward even as Cricket was spinning, spinning, spinning at the edge of the air. There was no John Brown. No Tubman. No Sees Her. Cricket's one good eye was open now, and bright, as if hanging restored rather than took away life. I got my breath and screamed, and he saw me: I don't imagine this, great-grandson, but know it for a certainty; his one opened eye caught mine in a look so unalarmed, so unhurt, so deep and forgiving and sweet that my terror departed me all of a sudden, in a rush; and I vomited all over the matty hair and smelly deerskins of the Kentuck who was holding me up. He yelled and dropped me like a camp potato. I hit on my feet and ran sideways through the crowd while they laughed, not at me but at their friend, who was shaking my vomit out of his greasy locks. I looked back once at Cricket to apologize for Brown and Tubman and myself, but Cricket was dead again, this time forever. Spinning slowly as he would spin forever. Home, I crept into the house and stole the ragged old quilt from the dog's bed behind the wood stove. I was shaking with fear and horror and hatred, like a fever, sick again. Mama called from out front, but I didn't answer. I went and hid in the barn and she came to find me. That night she told me my true, secret story: that Cricket was my brother, not my cousin, and that she was not my true mother but my aunt. (Thus, legally, I belonged not to Deihl but to old man Calhoun.) I didn't want to hear it. Shivering with rage and fever, I kept waiting for her to leave. That night the fire on the mountain burned as if nothing had happened, as cold and distant as a star. I hated it. I hated Brown. I hated Mama and even Cricket. I hated all black people.

November 1859
Miss Emily Pern
Queens Dispensary
Bath, England

Dear Emily:

I admit that I was as disappointed by the contents of your letter, as I was eager for its arrival. You say that you treasure *friends like me* far more than suitors, with their *wearisome declarations.* You are responding, though you are too kind to say it, to my overly bold confession the night before my duel. I was in the fevered state of the Condemned, and now I wish I had been either more, or less, direct.

But I will not apologize for *admiring* you.

So I reap my just reward: neither refused nor encouraged, a state appropriate indeed to my political position here.

I expected to be gone from here by Thanksgiving, but we won't make it. Our supplies were discovered and destroyed, even the wagon, and two of our number beaten by Copperheads; none killed. We must now replace it all. It is doubly difficult for me since I can perform no role in these events but must play the proper Virginia gentleman.

Things here in the City of Brotherly Love are violent and degraded by turns. Last night a mob of Copperheads raided a lecture by Mr. Martin Delaney (who has not held back from support for Tubman and Brown) but were beaten off by the "Friends of David Walker," a militia that includes a few whites as well as the free black longshoremen who are the stern guardians of Abolitionism in this city, and the main reason why the reactionaries have not carried the day.

Levasseur, since leaving for England two months ago, has fallen into a great Silence. Tell him, if you see him, he must write. We had twenty Englishmen here this week, calling themselves Charterists, disguised as immigrants for the Kansan Plain. Stout, both of principle and arms. Word is that a forty-five-ton sloop has been outfitted in Port-au-Prince for the Sea Islands of Carolina with munition, marines, and Toussaint's famed Jacobin Mule mountain cavalry. These are Haiti's best, and when they hit the South, God help slavery if indeed God loves it as much as the preachers illude. We hear that a brigade of Garibaldini are striking into Texas from Matamoras; they are expected to move North into what we call the South (and the Mexicans, el Norte) now that the *Republica* has been declared. There has been little fighting yet, the Texans apparently remembering the Alamo quite well, and in its true character, as a drubbing. Whether these Mexican Republicans intend merely to regain Texas or move deeper into the South is the question. In California, the Chinese, imported to slog the Railroads like the Irish here in the East, have joined with the Republicans, to re-raise the Bear Flag. The Irish in Baltimore are refusing to load tobacco for England. Emily, our dear Abolitionism has taken on an International as well as Revolutionary character!

The South is in a state of Alarm. There is next week a States' Rights Convention in Atlanta, called by those who think the federal government is not being forceful enough in defending slavery's prerogatives; they want to replace Lee with another, and are said to be raising an interstate militia, partly at least with English funds. My Uncle Reuben and my young Cousin Wm. Henry, his eldest surviving, are on their way, my father being too sick to travel.

My mother writes from Staunton that there's a hanging every week in every town, for as Lee can't get at Brown's army he makes his supporters (or supposed supporters) pay. I'm apprehensive about this trip even as I am anxious to go. My father is fast weakening. My sister is marrying the man who tried to shoot me, but flinched. They all assume, even my sister, that the war has cured my abolitionism (as with the few other liberal Southerners).

My thanks to Lee that his officers are little accomplished with small arms.

The great fear is of course that the Rebellion will spread beyond Virginia, which it has already begun to do. My cousin writes from Rumsey, in western Kentucky, that they no longer travel at night.

And you? And you? I promise, no more *declarations,* at least until a more appropriate circumstance; but please speak when he comes, to Levasseur, who *knows my heart better than any living man.* I will only make so bold as to *declare* that loneliness is my constant companion, with my true comrades so far from my side. I have friends in the Medical Ctte., but these Yanks are a New Breed, as cold a bunch as businessmen. There is, ironically, less friendship between black and white now than before the rebellion.

When next you hear from me I will be in Staunton. Has any man ever so dreaded going Home?

Yrs., &c., Thos.

☆ ☆ ☆

The first weeks of winter were desperate ones in the Shenandoah. Lee's forces occupied all the towns, and the Africans, free and slave alike, were treated as conquered souls; that always fine distinction between slave and free was seared away in the fire of war, and more and more there was only black and white. This seemed to chafe at Mama (for I still called her that) because she had always considered herself, *de facto* if not *de juris,* free, and she resented the arrogance of the soldiers quartered in our barn, even though they were guaranteed with federal money, far more reliable than the tobacco or timber vouchers of the militia. To me she explained that my true mother was her little sister, Taze, Cricket's mother, who had died giving birth to me. (That my father had run away, was true.) A bundle of rags had been buried alongside Taze to fool

old man Calhoun, and I had been spirited into town and given
to her sister, "Mama," who had been bought by Deihl and
promised freedom. He agreed to the deception. Cricket, who
was four, was told his baby brother had died with his mother.
I thought of the little grave with its constellation of colored
glass and stones: it was my own. This gave me a chill, like
discovering I was not born but awakened from the dead. When
Mama told me that Cricket had never been told the truth, for
the first time I cried, turning away from her, remembering his
big arm around me in the shadow of the willow. Why not? Had
they not trusted him, of all people, my own brother, who had
been butchered rather than say a word, rather than betray
either me or John Brown? Why was he never told? I was never
to find out. Mama never said, and Deihl and I never spoke of
such things. I turned away from Mama that day. In my anger
and grief (and arrogance), I told myself that with her own
relative freedom, such as it was, she had turned her back on her
own people. Though what was I but proof she hadn't? November went out cold and December came in wet. Deihl couldn't
find a buyer for the stable, so he and Mama worked like draft
beasts, and the money piled up. With Lee's winter campaign,
the "freedom" of the free Africans who made up a third of the
population of Charles Town (and almost half of Harper's
Ferry) was revealed in its true coin. We were under martial law.
The days when I could run wild through the streets and along
the river at any hour I liked were gone. Any dark face was
hailed, stopped, abused, and vilified at will by Lee's U.S. Marines, as often with a harsh Northern or even, God forbid, an
Irish accent as a Southern one. Meanwhile the Virginia militia
drilled and drank, and drank and drilled, confident in the illusion (later liberally swamped in blood) that they would not be
forced again to fight. By the time I looked up again, the Blue
Ridge above Charles Town seemed as lifeless as the moon. The

war seemed all but over. Brown on the run. Tubman, it was rumored, dead. And our condition worse even than before. I don't remember how I felt; I don't think I cared one way or the other, when they told me one night after dinner, a week and a half before Christmas, that we were leaving for Baltimore as soon as the weather broke. Old Deihl sat at the table, even took his hat off, pulled out his Bible, and recited (pretending to read) the verse about strangers in a strange land; then Mama laid fifty ten-dollar notes on the table and said he had sold the house and stable. I do remember that the stack of money and the Bible neither of them could read were precisely the same height.

☆ ☆ ☆

"I didn't mean to scare you," Harriet said, leaning back against her mother, who was leaning against a rock, which was leaning against a mountain, which was itself resting against the heart of that warm and welcoming planet, Earth. "I just wanted to see False Fire. I thought I would be back by the time you got back. Then it rained. I didn't realize the map was in miles. How come people ride klicks, but walk miles?"

"Feet are old-fashioned," Yasmin said. "Let's see your shoes. I just thought of something."

"Oh Mother, they're beautiful," Harriet said. "They really are." And they really were. The rain seemed to have brought the blues and grays to a swirling shimmer, like oil on water. The tops were higher and lighter, almost a moon color, and when Harriet touched them, they opened and fell into a little pool around her ankle. "Look, they've learned to undo themselves."

"Amazing," Yasmin said. She touched them, and they climbed back up again. "And the soles aren't so clunky now. See how soft they grow? You won't believe this, but I just remembered what it is you're supposed to do to make them grow in: get them wet. Go for a walk in the rain!

"So why were you crying? Is it the baby?"

Harriet shook her head. Her braids were ragged, Yasmin noticed. They definitely needed work. She felt that delightful old itching in her fingertips an African mother gets when she studies a daughter's hair. "You're sure you don't mind not being an only child?"

"Oh no."

"Positive?"

"No, I think it's great. The only thing is, I just wish . . ."

"Just wish . . ."

"I just don't want you moving to Africa. I was thinking about that. What would I do then? I don't want to change schools and . . ."

"Is that it?" Yasmin caught her daughter's chin and turned her head so she could look at her face. "Honey, I'm not moving to any Africa."

"Really? I thought you loved it so much, and now . . ."

"Is that why you never asked who the father was? I'm not even getting married. I'm just having a baby. In Charleston. At home. In our little yellow house. You and me."

"Really?"

"That's the fact, child."

Harriet thought this over. She grinned. She stood up and took her mother's hand.

"Well, I was just wondering, that's all," she said. "You took so long to come home."

They followed the winding path along the ridgetop, through brushy trees and laurel. The view they'd been promised from the rocks was gone now, and they might as well have been walking through a forest on the Valley floor. The path narrowed and Yasmin dropped back. Harriet was hungry. She wondered if her great-great-grandfather had ever walked this path. If she looked behind her, would she see him with the kids? Or would she see him in front with the grown-ups? Twelve and sixty at the same time. A kid with an old man's face.

"Did Great-Great-Grandpa ever come up here?"

"Probably not, except maybe digging sang with Cricket. But I don't think you find that on a mountaintop. By the time he joined Brown, they were a hundred klicks to the south," Yasmin said. "Almost to Roanoke."

"What's 'sang'?"

"Ginseng. He has a hospital named after him in Roanoke, and one in Ireland, too."

Harriet could always tell when her mother wanted her to ask questions. "Ireland? Really?"

"He fought with Connolly. That's a whole other story he never wrote. He left Nova Africa during the eighties, under a cloud. He went to Ireland where he met Connolly. That was the only actual fighting your great-great-grandfather ever did, against the British in 1885."

"What does that mean, 'under a cloud'?"

"Politics," Yasmin said. "Your great-great-grandfather was a revolutionary but not exactly a socialist, at least in his younger days—"

"But Nova Africa wasn't socialist then."

"It was headed that way." Yasmin didn't like to be interrupted. "—nor was he an easy man to get along with. It wasn't until after he came back from Ireland, in the late eighties, that he joined the Party. Even then, he argued with this one and that one until the day he died. But that's still another story. Are you hungry?"

"Starving."

"Grissom is waiting in the car on the road at Bear Pond Gap, where we were the other day when the car broke down. He says it's only a mile the other side of False Fire. But where is False Fire?"

The mountain was narrowing as it rose to the southward. The view was coming back, reluctantly. Through the trees on both sides now, they could glimpse golden fields of wheat far below. The trail wound up an easy rise, where the ridgetop got rocky again, then dropped slightly. Harriet ran ahead, then looked back and saw her mother, pregnant, but showing it only in how carefully she picked her way along the rocky trail.

"I found it," Harriet called back.

False Fire.

☆ ☆ ☆

December 20
Miss Emily Pern
Queens Dispensary
Bath
England

Dear Emily:

I got your letter one day and Lev's the next—learning from the one that he was wounded, from the other that he is in prison, from both that he is alive. Thanks be to whatever Entity it is that looks after Jacobins. He apologized to me, but I don't yet know what for, since apparently his letters have crossed in the mail. The mail-train robbery I had read of there, yet had no idea Abolitionists were involved, much less Lev! It was a bold stroke, the bolder since those who escaped got out of England with several hundred thousand pounds, I hear. Lev seems to think that, thanks to Marx's agita-

129

tion around the case, there is enough anti-slavery sentiment in England that he will serve no long prison term, and my hope is that he is right.

As for me, I am as you see by the weary address below, still in Philadelphia. I owe my unwanted leisure to unseasonable snow to the North and rain to the South of the Mason-Dixon line, which in terms of the weather has proved this year a most precise boundary, and fatal to our plan, since snow is sometimes kind to the traveler, but mud, never. We're hoping for a break in the weather after the New Year.

Was there ever a man so impatient to enter Purgatory?

> Your friend and Colleague,
> Thomas
> City of Brotherly Love

☆ ☆ ☆

I have no story to tell of Lee's great victory at Front Royal or his subsequent defeat at Winchester, or the rout at Strasburg. I witnessed none of it, yet I saw it all. The tides of war were reflected in the face of every white person, which changed like the oceans of a planet too familiar with its moon; while the black faces in the Shenandoah Valley were, through years of training, impassive and unreadable, often even to ourselves. After Deihl sold the house and stable, only the weather, the worst in many years, held us in Virginia. Many others were trapped as well; a sea of refugees, black as well as white, filled Charles Town, and every day we were lashed with rumors like sleet. The war didn't wait on the weather. On Christmas Eve we heard that Brown was encircled and all was lost (or won);

they had brought a rope from Kentucky to hang him with, donated by the hemp growers, and another more elegant noose of Sea Island cotton. The buckskins laughed and sang carols as they rode off with Lee's secondaries; they were followed by the militia, the Richmond Grays, eager now to join the fight they had until now been so satisfied to be left out of. None of them came back. Not one. In the morning we heard of the encirclement, and in the evening we heard of the "defeat." (For we n'Africans were still in another man's country, using his words backward. Even today, fifty years later, I catch myself rejoicing at a defeat and weeping for a victory.) But there was no hiding the smiles of the black folks when it was found out that not only Brown but Tubman lived; our gallant Tubman, it was in fact she who (as it later turned out, this had been planned) broke the encirclement with the first international detachment of Haitian cavalry, of Garibaldini in their red silks, of Cherokee and Creek warriors, and Pennsylvania Molly Maguires. The "Grays" were slaughtered, and I use the word with medical precision. The Carolina militia drowned in its own liquored-up blood. A few of the Kentucks and the Fourth Rhode Island got away. Meanwhile, to the south, Atlanta was burning, and the Cherokee courthouse raid had filled Asheville with troops, and emptied it of citizens. The South was calling for more troops, and the abs up North were agitating against them, even in the ranks. Like a fire, abolition was consuming the South. I had vowed to join Brown; then I had hated him; now I was eager to join him again. But the war had moved up the Valley from Charles Town, and I was only a twelve-year-old boy and an African, and there was no way I could head south without looking like a runaway slave. I resolved the conflict as I have resolved so many in my life: by numbing myself against it, working unthinkingly, waiting for the weather to break.

TERRY BISSON

☆ ☆ ☆

JAN 15 1860
MINT SPRINGS FARM
STAUNTON VIRGINIA

LAURA SUE HUNTER BEWLEY:

DELAYED BY WEATHER/ ARRIVING HOME WEEK OF
FEB 1/ AT LEAST THE WAR BROUGHT US A TELE-
GRAPH/ TELL FATHER HOLD ON/ LOVE THOS

Every year in the South there is a "Little Spring" toward the end of January, when the earth thaws out; the sun warms the air, if not the mud; and one feels almost as if the trees will be fooled into blooming. But only the people are. I was surprised to feel sorrow at leaving the old half-board, half-log house, and the stable where I had toiled so many hours for the horses I never grew to love: such are the attachments of childhood, which it is mistakenly said grow weaker through the years. It is years later, looking back from the barren mountaintop of age, when we feel most keenly the sorrow that childhood's continual state of leaving evokes. We loaded the wagon and drove past the gallows, but I couldn't find a tear to shed for my brother, or for myself. We rode across the Potomac bridge and past the steep wild end of Maryland Mountain, and I remembered the morning, it seemed a century ago, when I had seen that bold little army setting out. It had been the Fourth of July, deliberately, and now, for better or for worse, they had transformed every life in the valley. That July morning the road had been empty, but now it was crowded and we were part of a stream of humanity, all headed North. Thousands of others were seizing upon that break in the winter to flee Virginia and the war.

132

The road through the Gap to Frederick was cut off, so we followed the rest of the refugees north toward Hagerstown. Hundreds of people and wagons were bottled up a few miles north of the Potomac at Boteler's Ford on Antietam Creek. The ford had been gnawed away by the traffic and the waters, and an enterprising local family, the Cutshaws (whom we knew very well as mule sharpers) were making money "sailing" wagons across with ropes and oxhides filled with air. It was an odd scene, of the kind that war spawns. Antietam Creek was swollen with an unaccustomed flood, which even more than the warm air made it seem like spring. The south bank was crowded with humanity of all ages and both sexes, black and white, talking, smoking, laughing, cursing, watching with admiration the Herculean exertions of the four gigantic Cutshaw boys, who were thrashing the wagons across the creek. Women helped one another with the babies while boys and men helped the horses haul the wagons over the steep stones. The Africans were most of us women and children and the old, for once unmolested by the whites. The tension of the past months seemed eased by the struggle in the creek below, by the commotion of flight. Here two nations, which were forty miles to the south fighting one of the bloodiest battles of the war, were mingled in a peasant scene from Brueghel, rich with the humor and compassion with which our race is blessed: I mean our human race. It made me not resent war but credit it, for the ordinary day-to-day conflict of slavery admitted no such moments of humanity; and I was glad that "peace," at least, was gone forever, whatever the future might hold. Like the rest, I put my skinny shoulder to the wheel. The passage across the creek was slow. Everybody got wet along with the Cutshaws, who stayed wet and grimly energetic, with sticks and weeds tangled in their hair, like great yellow bird dogs. We were on the bank for ten hours. Every hour the news changed, from "Lee winning" to "Lee losing" back to "Lee winning." It seemed not to matter to the tide of

refugees. The whites were the small farmers, and a few of the
great ones who had recently discovered the virtue of looking
and acting like small ones. The Africans were the free blacks
and the abandoned or runaway slaves passing as free, all unchallenged and unquestioned, since the cash value of a human
being had dropped (that is, great-grandson, risen) almost to
nothing with the war. One would have thought, seeing that
crowd, that we n'Africans were a nation of children and boys,
women and old men; and I think it lent speed, on the one hand,
and heart, on the other, to the refugees to realize how many of
the able-bodied black men were "missing count"—that is, gone
Up the Mountain. We were all morning, then all afternoon on
Antietam Creek. Like the Cutshaws, Deihl and Mama saw a
chance to make a little money. Mama had me "hurry up" a fire
and she fried up some hoecake and boiled chicory, which she
sold at coffee prices to the people around, and to the people
coming through from the other side, where the line was of
course much shorter. In fact, only one wagon came over from
the North, although several horsemen—adventurers, military
contractors, newspapermen, and a few revolutionaries, I expect,
posing as all three—splashed across. This wagon was a brand-
new Pennsylvania Townerley driven by a youngish white man,
a doctor I later discovered, well outfitted, with a fair pair of
Morgans, one of which picked up a stone in the creek. I helped
him doctor it, and Mama sold him some hoecake. He seemed
a gentleman and had a fine pair of duelling pistols under the seat
of his wagon (I happened to notice), and I heard plantation
Virginia in his speech. That was when I got my idea. Much as
we dislike one another, horses and I have an understanding: this
doctor was having trouble with the Morgan that had picked up
the stone, and I calmed things out for him. He said I was pretty
good with a horse. "I loves horses," I told him, in that "nigger"
talk white folks love to hear, "and de Morgan de bestest." It

was growing dark by then, and I bid farewell to Mama, though God forgive me, were there one, she didn't know it. I told her and Deihl that I had made an arrangement to help the Cutshaw boys through the night for two dollars, and would catch up with them down the road, the traffic being so slow. Here was the cruelest act of my childhood. I was never to see Mama again, for she died of the pox that laid Baltimore low the third year of the war. I never even kissed her good-bye, not only because I was cold to her then (but I was! I was!) but because such a gesture might have given away my intention to head South. How often since that day have I remembered the love and care she gave me. I was to see old Deihl once more, in his old age, twenty years later, but it was strange between us without Mama, to say the least. She had left me some money, and he had tried to get it to me, but the U.S. government at that time wouldn't release funds for Nova Africa. The doctor made it past Charles Town and almost all the way to Winchester before he stopped to rest his horses and sleep. In the back of his wagon he found a twelve-year-old African stowaway curled up (and by now I was no longer pretending) asleep.

February 2, 1860
Miss Emily Pern
Queens Dispensary
Bath, England

Dear Emily:

Well, I am at last in Staunton, after a harrowing week's journey, during which I almost lost my horses, my chest, and my life; delivered a child (dead); was delivered by another; and gained an assistant and lost him again.

I suspect that even if you have written I will be late in getting your letters; so in the meantime, exiled in my own home as I am, let me share with you the scenes of terror and hope that have engulfed your country since you left. Every year in the South there is a Little Spring, late in January. This year it released me from my long wait. I left Philadelphia Thurs last and crossed the Mason-Dixon line into Maryland Friday, A.M., already west of the mountains. From Hagerstown on into Virginia, the highway was a scene of fantastic confusion and fear, though the terror really only began after Lee's defeat at Signal Knob. The road was filled with refugees, deserters, bandits, looters, the wounded, the abandoned, the quick and the dead—all heading North. There were few others heading south; we were often forced to the fields as the crowded road would simply not admit traffic in a southerly direction. I say We, for just south of Martinsburg, at a miniature Noah's flood called Antietam Creek, I was attached to by a slave boy of about fifteen, named Ayrab (I spell it as he pronounced it), who had been hired out to help drive cattle to Hagerstown and was now on his way back to Roanoke to rejoin his mother and master (he said). He had lost his traveling letters (he said) and was afraid of red-lighters and worse, and so attached himself to me, after helping with my Morgans. I felt the sting of delivering a slave back to his master, but hid my true feelings, since the boy helped me complete my own cover, and we agreed he would pass as my personal servant.

Ayrab had his race's knack with horses and more as well: for he helped me deliver a baby, or rather the mother, for the baby was beyond our Deliverance; and he later saved my life (as I will tell). The mother was a young Negress who had been cruelly left in a brush arbor behind a church just a half day south of Winchester; we heard her pitiable cries from the highway. Her child was born dead, the boy assisting me with a natural touch, for he had fear of neither suffering nor blood (essential in a doctor's helper); yet after the birth I saw he was not so stoic as I had imagined; for when I handed him the baby to put aside (I had given up on it) and help me clean up the girl, he wouldn't put it down, but cradling the dead infant in his arms, he burst into tears as if it had been his own. Nor would he leave without burying it, even though it was about to grow dark and the colored family who had agreed to take the girl North with them warned us of bandits, and not to remain in the shadows near the church. He buried the child African-style with a willow shoot on the grave. They often use a tree as a living headstone. He lay in the back of the wagon and cried himself to sleep as I drove south; I covered him with a blanket and drove on, and after a while he grew quiet.

It was only two hours later, after dark, ten miles up the pike, that he saved my life. We were far enough up in the valley now to see the famous fires—one on the Blue Ridge, one on Signal Knob, and two on the Cumberlands to the west. Emily, though they had altered my very life, I had never before seen them. Beautiful they were, like stars, and indeed they had drawn me here like the Christ star; and others from around the world, as well. I was musing on how very far they were visible (poetically), all the way from England, Italy, Greece, even Africa. We were heading across a muddy field of corn stubble, the road being clotted with northbound carts and horses, the winter being the wettest in many years, when a detachment of men hailed us. There were six of them, carrying pitch pine torches, mounted very well but poorly armed with government muskets, and the leader with a shotgun. The leader asked my destination, and I told him, Staunton. He was wearing a Lee cap, and I guessed that they were deserters. He asked my name and I told him, but the name Hunter seemed to inspire envy and hostility rather than respect.

He said: —Well, Mr. Hunter, we're looking for Yanks, abs, and deserters— —And stolen goods— he added, nodding toward my traps.

I knew then that their intention was to steal my new Townerley and everything in it. I hoped that they wouldn't see the young Negro covered with a blanket in the back, since they would probably take him for a runaway; but he had the presence of mind to stay covered. I regretted my folly in not being armed. I had only the two Longmann duelling pistols under my seat, and they were untouched since the infamous duel: still charged only with powder but no shot.

I said: —Carry on then, but you have no business with me— Meanwhile I reached under the seat, as if for my whip, edging toward the pistol case, figuring an unloaded weapon better than none, since they would at least make a flash and roar.

I clucked up the horses, but the man in the Lee cap impudently took my lead horse's bit and stepped into our path, the others by his side.

—Your papers, sir!— he said.

I found the pistol case with my fingertips, and answered him: —Papers?— (I said) —Gentlemen, it'll be a sorry day when a free-born Virginian shows papers to white trash that can't even read. Now you will either stand aside or regret it in Hell!—

—G–d damn you for a dog!— he bellowed and reached for the horses, just as I opened the case—and found it empty! My God, I am lost, I thought, falling back just as there was a blast in my ear and the Morgans reared in their traces.

I thought I had been shot, but it was our bandit who clutched his face as the Lee cap flew off his head; he fell and his shotgun went off, and I heard the load rip by me in the air, the second time I have heard that dreadful noise. Meanwhile (all this happening in the same instant), the Morgans bolted, throwing me down; and I looked behind me and I saw the Negro boy standing robed in the blanket like Hamlet's ghost, with my two pistols! The Morgans were running and the boy was thrown against the tailgate, my other gun in his hand discharging with a prodigious flash and roar. Behind us I saw the bandit's horse dragging him through a fence while the others tried to catch it.

There were more shots, but whether at us or the bandit's horse I could not tell, for we had regained the road and were careering like the wind. The boy joined me on the seat, a smoking pistol in each hand, still wrapped in my red blanket like a red Indian. I took back my guns and loaded them, this time properly with shot, while he drove. I couldn't determine how he had prevailed with unloaded weapons. Perhaps the powder blast and wad alone had scorched the bandit's face. At any rate, we reached Strasburg by midnight, beasts lathered, but safe. I was surprised to find blood had spoiled the shoulder of my coat; a shotgun pellet had torn my ear, but that was all.

Thus, my formal Introduction to war! It's too soon to wrote what Staunton is like; I have only been here a day. I am anxious to hear of yourself and Lev. Are his wounds healed? Are you able to visit him in Prison, and will he be brought to trial? Tell me, do you ever think of your old friends here? Write me freely at the old address in Phila. I have made arrangements to secure my mail.

> Yr. Brother in Sentiment and Determination,
> Thom

Here, on a ledge overlooking the valley, a great ring of stones were piled, still blackened by smoke after a hundred years. There was no plaque, no railing, no displays, no brochures, no guards or attendants; if you climbed the mountain and followed the ridgetop, you found it just as Brown and his men had left it one hundred years before, minus the roaring flames.

False Fire.

There was no plaque because everyone knew the story. Two men kept the great fire burning while Tubman and Brown moved their few precious soldiers south: not through Key's Gap, where Lee's pickets were expecting them, but down the steep hollows into the Valley, across the Shenandoah in ones and twos and fours and tens, then south to Signal Knob: the whites disguised as preachers, newspapermen; the blacks as corn pickers, slaves on hire slouching from farm to farm through the long rows. Once twelve men together were disguised as two slave brokers with a coffle of ten "bucks" for the Georgia turpentine plantations. They had left behind only two to tend the fire; and of these one managed to escape and rejoin them, because he was white, passing himself off as a major's

140

aide who had followed the troops up the mountain out of curiosity; the other was shot and then suffocated in the tunnel he had designed for escape.

"Two men," Yasmin said. "And Lee sent a thousand."

She stood beside her daughter on the still-blackened stones and watched the valley drying in the sun a thousand feet below. Here, out of the trees at last, there was a feeling of height. Harriet loved it: just to stand there was to soar. Yasmin didn't like it. She had never shared Leon's love for emptiness. She sat down, weak in the knees. They could see up the valley to Harper's Ferry, and west to Charles Town. To the east, across the low top of the mountain, they could see Hillsborough and Mechanicsville in the Loudon Valley. Far to the south an airship was motoring easily northward in the lee of the mountain.

Yasmin could almost hear the high singing in her bones. "Now don't be jumping around here," she said. The sun was dropping through the clouds over the Cumberlands, and Grissom was waiting for them in her car at the Gap, but Yasmin didn't want to go. Let him wait. This was the first time she had felt at peace with her daughter in a year.

Getting up her courage, she leaned out a little and looked down. It wasn't a straight drop, just a long rocky slope. She threw a stick and listened to hear it hit . . .

"I shouldn't have waited three days to tell you. With all the Mars stuff, I guess I was thinking about your father and all. I mean, he probably would think . . . ."

"Mother, he's dead."

"Well."

"No, I mean really. Actually dead. He's not up there wondering what you're doing. Honestly, sometimes you sound like Grandma."

"Probably you're right. Anyway, I didn't even think of getting married when I met Ntoli," Yasmin said. "He's not like your father, he's a wanderer. He can't stay in any one place."

Who could be more of a wanderer than my father? Harriet thought. But she knew enough about her mother not to interrupt. So she sat down and laid her head on her lap, gradually, gingerly: while Yasmin told Harriet the story of how they'd met in Dar while she had been cataloguing the Olduvai Project. Ntoli was the brother of one of the other women on the project; he was an agronomist home from a project in Holland, on his way to a conference at U.N. headquarters in Jerusalem. A world traveler. A sweet man with doe eyes who spoke four languages, none of them English. And almost ten years younger. "My Xhosa and Arabic are both so bad," Yasmin said, "that we laughed a lot and hardly ever argued. I didn't intend to get pregnant. But when I did, I was glad." She looked down at her daughter on her lap. "It seemed to make sense."

"What did he think?"

"Oh, he doesn't know."

"What?"

"I didn't tell him."

"Mother!"

Yasmin grinned wickedly. "I will. After. Maybe. Of course. But first I had to talk with you. Not to mention your grandmother. Not to mention our collective back in Charleston. You see, child, Ntoli is a very lovely man, but I have no intention of marrying, least of all a man that much younger. Anyway, it was all an accident and he was already on his way to Palestine when I found out . . ."

Harriet heard a high, joyful singing in her head; she looked over without sitting up and saw the blue and silver *Tom Paine* passing just a few hundred feet away. There was silence like the eye of a storm as the ship passed, the plasma motors sounding farther away the closer they were.

Harriet loved airships, and seeing the ship pass so closely, actually looking slightly down on it, made her feel lucky, like walking up on a deer. Watching from her mother's lap, she felt lucky twice. Without sitting up, she waved at a small face on the glassed-in rear deck, going away: a little girl, alone, looking back as little girls do. She wouldn't mind having a baby brother. She was just glad to have her mother back. She laid her head back down on her mother's lap and looked up.

"I bet you're scared about telling Grandma."

"Of course not. Well, sort of. But mainly, I wanted to tell you first."

"Really?" Yasmin smiled to watch Harriet wiggle with delight. "Still, she'll be shocked! When you going to tell her, Mama?"

"Tomorrow."

"Promise?"

"We'll be at her house to watch the Mars landing. I'll tell her then; then it's back to Nova Africa for us."

"I bet she'll think you should get married."

"And move to Africa? Or Palestine? I think not. She wouldn't want that any more than you. Or me. Besides, she's religious and old-fashioned, it's true, but she's not really so narrow-minded as you think. Leon could talk her into anything. Even into me."

"What do you mean, Daddy could? Tell me."

Yasmin laughed. "You should have seen the first time he brought me home to Staunton. I was definitely what you might call a radical, at least for Virginia."

"What do you mean? Tell me."

"I mean, there I was coming from a big university in Nova Africa. A genuine communist. I had long dreads and big-city shoes. I was vice president of the Pan African Friendship League—that's how I met your dad. (We worked with all the cute foreign students!) But seriously, Pearl thought all that was the Devil's work. Remember, this was 1943, '44. Before the Revolution here, and a lot of the black folks in the U.S.— especially in the country, like your grandmother—were pretty old-fashioned. The younger folks like your father were looking south of the border; that's why he went to school in Nova Africa in the first place instead of the U.S. So anyway, there we were home for his Christmas vacation. I was in the U.S. illegally, and—"

"So what did she say? What did she do?"

"Your grandma? She cut me some pie. I think it was chess pie. I think she thought that would straighten me out."

"What did Daddy do? What did he tell her?"

"Oh, him! He didn't have to say anything. He got what he wanted with that damn lopsided grin of his. Nothing was too good for her boy. He was an only child."

"Like you."

"Like you."

"Not anymore. I'm going to have a baby brother, remember?"

"Quit saying that, Harriet. How do you know it's going to be a boy. That might be bad luck."

"I just have a feeling." Harriet laughed, looking up. Her mother's face loomed close, like a dark, warm moon. "Do you ever have conjure dreams?"

Harriet felt her mother stiffen, and for a moment she thought maybe she had said the wrong thing.

"Hello!"

Harriet sat up.

Three figures were stepping out of the trees into the fading sunlight: three Mericans, two of them with big packs and rain hats that looked, for only a heartbeat, like space suits.

"Hello, we just heard it on the radio, we're on Mars! The *Lion* has landed."

Alarming even herself, Yasmin burst into tears.

144

Doc, for that is what he had me call him, and I beat south for
two days, using the roads when we could and the fields when
we couldn't. I had not yet passed from the shrewd clarity of the
old child into the ignorant opacity of the young man, so I knew
that Doc was not exactly what he seemed, though I didn't
suspect that he was an actual abolitionist—the same surgeon I
would later serve as assistant On the Mountain. He was even
blinder than I, though. I had fooled him into thinking that I was
good with horses; all that remained was to fool the horses,
which was not difficult. The first morning out of Charles Town,
he saved me from paddy rollers by posing as my master, the role
of the Virginia gentleman coming pretty easy to him. The country was filled with bandits. In Winchester, I watched several
thugs eye the wagon, which was filled with costly medical
supplies—which I was determined to steal myself and deliver,
somehow, to Brown and Tubman; as a hero, though I hadn't
quite worked out the details. The irony was that the Doc was
delivering them to the rebels himself, but I didn't know that.
That morning while the Doc was relieving himself (in a thicket:
the Virginia gentleman), I double-loaded his two pistols, which
were already primed and loaded, with a handful of insurance
(gravel) and tamped them with a biscuit, following Cricket's
trick, which had saved me once and was to serve again. That
afternoon the Doc delivered a child, with me helping. He had
a gentle way about him. The mother was little more than a child
herself, and it was extremely sad; the baby born dead. A boy.
I was right to expect bandits; I was, as it happened, napping
under a blanket in the back of the Townerley when a gang
stopped us. I woke to hear the Doc trying to bluff them down,
but with little success. Peeking out from under the blanket, I
counted four, in torchlight. I had removed the pistols from their
walnut case, and when the bandit leader made his move, I fired

145

into his face, which was lighted with a torch. He screamed (all the men I killed that year screamed) and fell backward with his boot twisted in the stirrup. Our Morgans lunged forward, and I fell. In the moonlight I could see the bandit's horse dragging him through a downed fence of that new barbwire from Baltimore that was going up all over the Valley, then stopping for the others. There were no shots from them, and no further pursuit, my guess being that they were not real highwaymen but soldiers, plundering and less than anxious to be discovered. At the same time they dropped behind us, so did the night, and it was dawn, or at least its beginning, dawn's dawn. The Doc was bleeding from a torn ear but exhilarated. So was I. I had killed another man, and so far, great-grandson, I liked it.

March 10, 1860
Miss Emily Pern
Queens Dispensary
Bath, England

Dearest Emily:

My father died last week, after a lingering illness. It is one benefit of my Work here that I am on hand to deal with the family business in a way that leaves the others free to express their Sorrow. I am now master of Mint Springs. The event is one of war's ironies: I can no longer manumit my slaves since that would endanger my Work here. However, they have manumitted themselves, leaving us only with the old and infirm. Human souls are of no cash value in the Valley any more.

I miss Philadelphia more than I suspected I would.

The same forces of war and revolution that have made Staunton an intellectual and moral Graveyard, are making Philadelphia shine and soar. According to my contacts still there, not since Byron's days in Greece has one seen so many international adventurers, revolutionists, reformers, and sundry Idealists in one seaport. I hear New Orleans is even more exciting, having risen like Paris in '48 and detached itself from the inland regions when the Quarter took arms. The poet Whitman has gone South to join Brown, and the main body of Garibaldini are heading north across Texas. In Concord, Emerson and Thoreau are not speaking, having ignited their own Civil War to match the one raging through the Abolitionist movement in general. *Viva la revolución!*

An added irony: the young Negro, Ayrab, who saved my life, has run away, stealing one of my matched pistols given me by my father, rendering the set worthless.

Emily, life here is bleak. I don't exactly miss my father; we were not close: but I miss having one. Politically, I find myself fearing discovery almost less than Success, which commits me to an endless solitary clandestinity, even while attending dismal rounds of socials and patriotic balls, cloaked like the whole town in mistrust and dread. People here never look up, fearing what they will see: the beacon fire on the Blue Ridge to the east; another on the Cumberlands to the west. It's like being afraid of the stars. There have been four raids on Lee's pickets in the past two weeks, and after each the Federals say the raiders were caught. Most ominous of all, last week they hanged a white man, a trader from Tennessee accused of selling horses to the abs, for gain rather than politics. (All the more portentous, Amer-

147

ica!) From here the fire on the mountain dominates heaven. I alone of the whites in Staunton look up—but secretly. I have already had some success in getting medical supplies up the mountain.

In the meantime I am warned that certain forces are inquiring about me, perhaps tipped off by their sources in Philadelphia to my secret role here. Ironically, my Uncle Reuben defends me, as a reformed idealist. And who could be more Trustworthy than the Master of Mint Springs, who waits in secret for word of his loved ones. Of Lev? And of Emily?

> Your Faithful and Affectionate,
> Thos &c. &c. &c.

March 27, 1860
Mrs. Emily Levasseur
Queens Dispensary
Bath, England

Dear Emily:

The betrayals of Destiny and the vagaries of the mail in a country torn apart by war are such that I got your letter and Lev's, written three weeks apart, on the same day. What is more tragical, to lose a heart's desire, or two friends at one blow? What is more loathsome, his apologetics or your justifications? The fact that he was in Prison until recently partly explains his long silence; but yours? A little honesty might have saved me much humiliation, if that ever entered your calculations. I return herewith your few letters. Farewell.

> Thos. Hunter, Esq., M.D.
> Mint Springs Farm
> Staunton, Virginia

☆☆☆

The third Merican was Grissom. He hadn't felt like waiting in the car. The two hikers had to get to the campground by the Potomac before dark, but they couldn't just walk away from a crying woman. Not knowing what else to do, the older of the two opened a pocket on his teenage son's pack and took out a burgundy-colored foil blanket, shaking it out of a package smaller than itself. He handed it to the one-legged man, who wrapped it around the heaving shoulders of the n'African woman sobbing loudly on the blackened ring of stones overlooking the Shenandoah Valley.

Grissom sat down beside Yasmin as Harriet was kissing her mother's cheek and getting up.

"That's a real space blanket," said the boy to Harriet. "Is that your mother? Do you want some club soda?"

"Help me build a fire," Harriet said. "She's crying for my father. He was killed on the first Mars voyage."

"I see," said the boy's father, looking wonderingly from her, to Harriet, to Grissom, who nodded.

"It's okay," Harriet said. "It's time to cry. I already cried. It was a long time ago."

The boy looked at Yasmin, amazed. "Was he the Lion?"

"He sure was."

It was getting cold. In October the warmth of the day goes quickly with the sun, which was almost touching the low blue wall of the Cumberlands far to the west. Yasmin stopped crying; she looked around and saw Harriet behind her, piling up sticks with the boy.

Grissom was sitting beside her, examining his boot, rolling his foot around inside it. "The problem with a one-legged man is, he gets all his blisters on one foot," he said.

Yasmin started crying again.

149

Grissom put his arm around her. *Jesus,* he thought. "I'm sorry you missed watching the landing with your ring-mother," he said.

"Oh it's probably all right. I'll be there tomorrow. We'll watch them put the plaque down. We'll have a good cry."

"Promise, comrade?"

She laughed. "Promise, comrade. I can't believe you walked here."

"It's not that far, really, from the car. I saw these guys cross the road and grabbed my crutches and followed. You know I hiked from Quebec to Nova Africa twice; the doctors tried to get me to keep it up after the war. But it's not the same."

"I wouldn't think so."

"But you miss it. But you know about missing things." He stood up and reached for her hand. "Right?"

"Right."

"Plus, a one-legged man gets all his blisters on one foot."

"You already said that."

"So? You want to talk about something else, comrade?"

Yasmin laughed. She stood up and folded the space blanket and returned it to the boy's father.

"You were right to criticize me for playing the old lady's game," Grissom said.

"You're right I was right. Class struggle doesn't stop just because folks get old and pitiful. Plus, she wasn't so damn senile."

"I think the museum makes me greedy."

Yasmin observed with a new, still unsteady calm that it was actually getting dark.

"I'm starving," she said to Grissom.

"I brought the sandwiches from the car."

In front of her, thirty klicks across the Valley, she could see the disappearing sun painting the clouds and the tops of the Cumberlands with fire. It was a little late to be wondering if she was still afraid of the dark. Behind her she could hear Harriet breaking sticks.

It was no easy thing to join the Army of the North Star, at least not in the spring of 1860. My ambition was to be a guide as Cricket had been, but without Mama and Deihl I was without a cover, and in Staunton I lacked the mobility I'd had in Charles Town. After helping the Doc for a few weeks with his horses, I said my farewells (not in his hearing) and made my way back north toward Charles Town. Since Brown was moving his troops toward Winchester in what white folks hoped and Lee thought would be the decisive battle of the war, the famed "Winchester Feint," the traffic north was lighter and the paddy rollers not so bold. Having learned that the only safe place for a "colored" boy in the Shenandoah in 1860 was in the company of a white man, I attached myself to a German journalist, a Marxian socialist who taught me in two days a habit it took me thirty years to overcome: snuff. I still miss it. Like Tubman, I carried my pistol (I had left one of the pair for the Doc) in a tow sack, like trifles. The troops were thick around Winchester, so I went all the way to Charles Town with my German, then remained while he headed back South, still looking for his story. Like Lee, I had missed Brown again. The army, and Lee's hope for a decisive victory, had disappeared even as Lee encircled it (leading folks to call it the Army of the Morning Mist that spring). For the next few weeks the soldiers took out their frustration on the few Africans left around, so I laid low for six days and nights, living in Deihl's still unoccupied livery barn on a ham I swiped from a neighbor's smokehouse. I still can't eat country ham. Here I was back where I had started. I had a gun but no money or food, and no idea of where to go. The hurricane lamp on the wall, the calling of the night birds, made me miss Cricket more. It was March, great-grandson, and cold. I succeeded through dumb luck, as I sometimes do. After a week in the barn, I decided to head South again, and even though it wasn't on the way, I went out to Green Gables to visit Cricket's grave. The home house at Green Gables had burned, and all the slaves had either run away North, been sold South, or gone Up the Mountain. I cut through the canebrake to the secret site of the graves of Brown's men. They were neglected, and I raked them with a bush and straightened the area. Then I went to look at my own grave and Cricket's, side by side. I was so cold and lonely that I welcomed my grief like a friend, wrapping my arms around myself. "Well, Cricket, what now?" I said, the first words I had spoken out loud in six days. Then I saw some money! Cricket's grave, like mine, had been decorated with bottles, and one of his contained four fifty-cent pieces. They had to have come from Mama. I counted them out, kept two and put two back to be fair, then took one more for myself since Cricket was dead and I wasn't, not yet anyway. To make it up to him, I split the colored stones he'd put on my grave between mine and his. Just then, darkness covered me like a cloud and arms trapped me from behind. I fell to the ground, not daring to scream, my first, unbidden thought being that it was Cricket's ghost. Then I smelled the harsh smell of unwashed men, and I knew I was done for. But these didn't smell like white men. Without a word they took my gun and my money. I was still pretty small for my age, and I was pulled headfirst into a tow sack and thrown over a mule, still without a word. "Help," I said, which is a foolish thing to say to your captors. Then a black voice clucked and said, "Up, Jen," and we were moving through the canebrake. "Help," I said again. A thick, black old man's voice dark as sorghum, and as sweet, and as slow, said: "Honey, you with the Army of the North Star now, so hush that racketness up."

152

July 10, 1862
Dr. Emily Levasseur
Queens Dispensary
Bath, England

Dear Dr. Levasseur:

You don't know me, I am the sister of the Late Dr. Thomas Hunter, Esq., of Mint Springs, Staunton. I know of you because he confided once to me of his great Admiration for you and that you were friends. I am writing this to let you know, unfortunately, that Thomas is dead: a Rebel, as you know, he was killed at the Second Battle of Roanoke, where they say he had stayed behind to help the Wounded and is buried in our family graveyard, G.R.H.S., with his Father and our cousin Johnny, also killed in the War. Even though he had left the Bosom of his Family, he is Missed by all those who knew and loved him; it is truly His most pure whom God calls Home.

> Sincerely, in Sorrow
> but Trust for God's Grace,
> Laura Sue Hunter Bewley

☆ ☆ ☆

"There was only one place to go," Grissom said. "South. Follow the ridgetops. Later they slipped east, across the valleys, as well. By the spring of '60, the fires appeared on other mountaintops, to the west, to the east, so that no one was quite sure where the Army of the North Star was hiding. But at first it was just a few men, and just one fire, right here."

153

"But how could they move a whole army without people knowing?" Harriet asked.

"There weren't as many of them at first as people thought. At most fifty. Usually less."

"So how could they beat Lee?"

"They couldn't," Grissom said. "That's why they were so careful never to fight him. Small groups they could beat, even when they were outnumbered."

"They knew the land better . . ."

"No, not really," Grissom said. "That's another myth. Remember, these were abolitionists from the North, a few n'Africans but mostly whites, and runaway slaves who had never had the mobility to know the country well. No, at first their enemy knew it better: the local whites, the hillbillies. They knew it well enough to know that once up on the mountain, Brown's men would be hell to get off. No, they were hard to fight because they had better weapons. Higher ground. And less to lose."

"And more to win," Yasmin added.

It was dark. She stirred the fire Harriet had built, and she could almost imagine that the sparks that flew upward were what was filling the rapidly darkening sky with stars.

"The Mericans wipe out the buffalo, string the country together with railroads and barbwire; annihilate, not just defeat, the Sioux, the Crow, the Cheyenne, the Apache, one after the other. Genocide is celebrated by adding stars to the flag. The Cherokee and the Creek languish in Oklahoma, stripped of their land. Settlers run the Mexicans out of California and Texas, or turn them into serfs, and move north to Alaska and south into the Caribbean, eventually seizing the entire continent . . ."

"Gross," said Harriet.

"Ridiculous!" said Yasmin. "The author would have all of

history hanging on one strand of rope with poor old Captain Brown."

"Oh, I agree," Grissom said. "It's a white nationalist fantasy, and somewhat overdone. But you must admit, *John Brown's Body* gives food for thought. What if the war had been started not by the abolitionists but by the slave owners? The political balance of forces was pretty precarious in the 1850s. What if the war had been fought to hold this nation together, instead of to free yours?"

"But the whole continent? That's ridiculous," Yasmin said. "The rest of the world, especially the League, wouldn't let that happen."

"There's no League in the book. In *John Brown's Body* there's no socialist Africa—it's all broken up into colonies of Europe."

"No Paris Commune? No English Civil War? No Russian, no Egyptian revolution?"

"I'm telling you. Socialism exists, but only as a threat. The world is basically ruled by the same people who built the railroads and the textile mills—British and then Merican capital. For a hundred years. And on into the future, until the end."

Harriet shivered and threw another stick onto the fire. "That's why I don't like science fiction. It's always junk like that. I'll take the real world, thanks."

"The funny thing is, it doesn't make them happy," Grissom said. "The Mericans, I mean. Having taken over the world, they turn on each other. They gorge on fat. They eat their own children. For a white supremacist fantasy the book has a certain grim honesty. It ends in this hideous. . . ."

"Please," Yasmin said. "I think I'll pass. John Brown the traitor, huh?"

"Worse; a madman. A murderous fanatic. Lincoln, on the other hand, is a hero. The great emancipator."

"Who does he emancipate?"

"Me," Grissom laughed. "He emancipates the whites from having to give up any of the land they stole. From having to join the human race."

"And Lee?"

"He survives the war, and loses it. But he sits a horse well. Speaking of which—I notice your daughter's living shoes finally came around to looking good. What was it, the rain?"

☆ ☆ ☆

Feb. 12, 1876
Mrs. Laura Sue Hunter Bewley
Mint Springs Road
Staunton, Virginia

Dear Mrs. Bewley:

Perhaps you will recall writing to my wife, Emily Pern Levasseur, some fourteen years ago on the occasion of the death of your brother, Dr. Thomas Hunter. I am returning your letter along with his correspondence with my late wife, who died last month after a long illness. These letters were among her most valued possessions, and I feel they should be in your family now, forming as they do a partial portrait of a brave and generous soul. Thomas Hunter was a friend of mine as well as hers, and even though events came between us, I am honored to have called him my comrade. Also, these letters reflect more on the destiny of your country (and its new neighbor, Nova Africa) than on this fog-shrouded Albion where I find my exile.

Sincerely,
R. Levasseur
Plymouth, England

✩ ✩ ✩

"The Jacobin outlived most of his comrades," Grissom said. "It's not in the letters, but I researched it. He was wounded twice—first in England, as part of a group robbing a mail train to finance a ship for the Sea Islands. He must have made it because later, in the siege of Atlanta, he lost a leg. I don't know which one. With legs it doesn't much matter."

"How'd he die then?" Yasmin leaned against Grissom's shoulder, half listening. Behind them, Harriet was breaking sticks and fiddling with the fire, enjoying the comfortable feeling of grown-ups ignoring her.

"The Commune. Paris, 1879. After Emily died, he managed to get to Italy, then France. He was with the Internationals when they broke the encirclement. Even with one leg. Probably driving a wagon."

It was growing cold. A thousand feet below, Yasmin could see the Valley looking cold and peaceful in the October moonlight.

Above it were the stars, which she hadn't looked at in five years, since Leon hadn't come back. Well, there they were. She looked straight back at them. They still looked like a graveyard, but that didn't bother her so much now.

She came from a people who knew about graveyards. Yasmin thanked the old doctor, Abraham, for bringing her up here. She kept her eyes closed and imagined him walking with her between the graves in a dream—what had Harriet called it, a conjure dream? He was old and young at the same time. A kid with an old man's knowing silence. They held hands, looking at the family graves, and it was as it should be. There was Cricket's, decorated with half the pretty stones. There was his own. There was Leon's with its black plastic plaque, and another little baby grave under a willow tree. They all three cried a little, looking down at that unknown one. Yasmin squeezed his hand in her waking dream and told him it was good to cry. I'm having another baby, Leon, she whispered out loud. The only one you and I had turned out pretty good. I miss you. Didn't you know I would? Like a fool she was crying again.

"Mama."

Yasmin looked up. Grissom's hand felt old in her own. In the firelight across from her, Harriet looked like her great-great-grandfather's oil portrait at Douglass Medical Center, lacking only the gray hair and the stiff blue suit. Allowing for her Daddy's humorous oak-brown eyes.

"Mama."

There was the little fire in her belly again.

"Mama, we want to go down," Harriet said. She stood up with Grissom and brushed herself off by the fire. The two of them had cooked up a plan. Harriet wanted to see the fire from the valley, so she had piled up wood. The plan was to throw it all on the fire at once, then hurry down the mountain in time to look up and see it blazing.

"During the Centennial," Grissom said, "you should have seen it then. We kept it burning every night for a week. We shouldn't really be doing this now, with no one to watch it. But look how wet it is."

"Let me give you two a head start," Harriet said. "Then I'll throw all the wood on and catch up."

Yasmin held the flashlight for Grissom, who swung speedily along the path on his crutches. He moved pretty good for an old man, she thought. She could hear Harriet racing to catch up. They reached the car in record time, and Grissom got into the driver's seat without being asked.

"Mama?"

Yasmin, getting into the car, turned and saw Harriet outlined in the dash light, still out of breath from the run through the woods.

"I'm not saying it's going to be a boy, Mama. But if it is, let's name him Cricket."

Te-oonk.

"Oh, no!" Grissom said. The starter motor made a dying sound. The engine rattled like broken crockery.

"Get in, Mother," Harriet said. "You're pregnant."

There was no time to waste, if they wanted to see the fire; and there was no point in worrying about the car. Luckily, it was already turned around. Harriet got it rolling easily and then jumped in, out of breath and laughing. Grissom went easy on the brake, and when they hit the straight stretch leading to Iron Bridge they were doing over 100. As they raced across the bridge, Grissom took something off the dashboard and sailed it out the window, into the Shenandoah River.

"What was that?" Harriet asked.

"Was that what I thought it was?" Yasmin asked.

It was. Grissom grinned. The book was gone. "She should have known better than to leave it with me," he said.

"Slow down!" Yasmin said. "You're passing the shop."

But instead of pulling in at Cardwell's, Grissom let the car roll on by, out of the trees, onto the westbound Charles Town road. They rolled to a stop in the wheat field. Yasmin remembered what they wanted to see, and she got out of the car with Grissom and Harriet; and they all three looked back and up together.

There it was, on top of the ridge, blazing. Like a star.

November 16, 1880
Mrs. Laura Sue Hunter Bewley
Mint Springs Road
Staunton, Virginia

Dear Mrs. Bewley:

The enclosed letter was written but never sent, on the eve of your brother's death at the Second Battle of Roanoke. When it was found among certain effects that turned up in Atlanta this year, it fell to me to try and find its intended recipient, as I had been your brother's orderly and, one might say, apprentice, as well as his closest companion in his last year. Since Mrs. Levasseur had died, and her husband disappeared, I thought the letter should devolve to your family, even though our nations are again at war, as it is the legacy of a warm and generous heart, who, though estranged from his country, never forgot his love for his family, and in particular the little sister of whom he often spoke with uncommon pride and warmth.

I was privileged to call him my friend, though there were twelve years between us.

My best wishes to you and your family.

> Yours truly,
> Dr. A. Abraham, M.D.
> Vesey Memorial Hospital
> Atlanta,
> Nova Africa

* * *

160

May 30, 1862
Dr. Emily Levasseur
Queens Dispensary
Bath, England

Dear Emily:

I hope you are not too surprised, or sorry, to hear from me. Greetings to you both (though I have written separately to Lev). If this reaches you, please know that I am recovered from my Sorrow, apologize for my Rage, and greet you as a Comrade.

I have been with the Army of the North Star now for almost two years, since my "practice" in Staunton came to a swift and almost fatal end. I was betrayed by my own uncle, Reuben, who was motivated as much by the desire for my property as patriotism; and I was saved by young Bewley, the very brother-in-law who had once tried to kill me; whose love for my sister and genuine horror at the War overcame his weakening federalism. As one of Lee's line officers, he knew and warned me of their plans. A gothic ending to a family tragedy, *non?*

Such are the fortunes of a civil war, which is what the Africans' Independence War has become for us Americans, as more and more whites who didn't have slaves either join or support the rebels for their own reasons, usually having to do with land. In fact, my uncle is one of the few who gained, instead of kept, a plantation by supporting Lee!

Emily, I was with old Brown when he died, a rare privilege. I'm now setting up a field hospital even as the war moves toward the West, with help from the Haitians and a brigade from England, raised by the communist Marx, whose doctrines, though industrial,

161

fall on fertile soil here. The youth who stole my gun
turned up again and has served two years as my apprentice, a young man with as sure a hand for medicine as he had for horses; I have made arrangements
to bring him here to help in the hospital, and have
undertaken to encourage him to study medicine seriously. He has made a lengthy passage along with the
rest of his people, from slavery to a new nation, independent, with liberty and justice for (truly) All.
Though still embattled, the government of Nova
Africa has now been recognized by several of the
Latin American powers; a newly freed Cuba and
Puerto Rico have welcomed it into association, along
with Eloheh, the government-in-exile of the Cherokee
who joined us south of the Smoky Mountains. The
Queen of England and the Chancellor of Germany be
damned, there are delegations of working men here
from both countries, building as well as fighting.
Charleston is now a polyglot sea of strange faces and
a beacon of new hope to the hemisphere. Meanwhile,
California has rejoined Arizona, Arizona has rejoined
Texas, and Texas has sent the Kentuckians packing
and rejoined revolutionary, republican Mexico. I was
twenty-six last month. I thought of you. I was in
Charleston, first capital of Nova Africa, picking up
medical supplies shipped from France, and witnessed
the disembarking of the 2nd Haitian Brigade, their
crimson cotton scarves fluttering in the southern
breeze. And Emily, though I was one of only two
hundred white faces in a cheering crowd of two thousand black ones, when I looked up and saw that now
familiar green and black and red flag, I got a feeling I
had never had in the Virginia that nurtured, or the
Philadelphia that liberated me. I was home.

I wish that every man and woman could know that feeling at least once. I sincerely wish it for you and Lev.

I write to you both now, on the eve of a great battle, for we are surrounded in Roanoke (for the second time), and our retreat has been not very successful. Who knows what tomorrow may bring; but I fear the worst, as always. I wrote you twice on such occasions before, remember? Once on the eve of a duel, and once before heading South to Staunton. I think no man thinks of death more than I. I both despise and honor it, for it silences the very heart it bids to speak. Emily, I'm sorry. Whatever disappointment you might have given me, your friendship (and Lev's) gave my soul so much more, by liberating me from a "peace" fatal to Love itself. And so, for the third time, in a word,

> Farewell.
> Your Affectionate Comrade and Friend,
> Thos Hunter, M.D., &c., &c.

☆ ☆ ☆

Yes, great-grandson, I was there the day old John Brown died. I was honored to be one of the six chosen to bury him on a mountaintop, and sworn never to tell which one: which is why it is said that every Appalachian peak is his grave. He was sixty-two, and he'd taken a minie ball in the side of the head in the fighting at Sugarloaf. Doc Hunter had treated him for two months, but Doc told me that the ball was in the brain (under the dura), and even though the wound might heal he would never get better. He was like a stroke victim, but declining every day, seized occasionally by trembling rages and weeping fits, totally uncharacteristic of the man. He had lost by then all but one of his sons, Watson, who joined him but was not recognized. His wife was dead; his daughters scattered by the Copperhead mob that had razed his North Elba farm. In these last days, Captain Brown turned the pages backward in his Bible. General Tubman pleaded with the Doc to try everything, for she herself suffered from seizures due to a wound to the head, but hers were of a less severe order, and after a while even she gave up. It was she, and not Douglass, who gave the order that the old man be helped to die, that his dignity might not pass away before his mortal body. I was no longer a boy, but fifteen and a veteran of three years of war: and as an orderly and, one might say, apprentice, I was privy to every medical secret. Tubman, that odd measure of oak and willow, strength and softness, gave the order, then left, then came back. Douglass was with us in those days, having just returned from New Orleans where he had been treatying with the new rulers of the city; this was when forces were pushing them to unite with pseudo-republican France rather than revolutionary Nova Africa, and he feared this cabal, but principle prevailed over capital and it faltered. This was in our first flush of victories— we had taken Roanoke and the Sixth Column under Green (actually the second but denominated as sixth to confuse the enemy) was even then poised to spring on Atlanta like the Black Panther after which it was named. We had bad times to come, great-grandson—the fierce winter of '63 was still ahead of us, when the Brits entered the war on the side of the Yanks and we lost Green's army and much of the land we had taken; but win or lose, it was a contest and we were no longer a little band on a mountaintop avoiding all encounters. We were an army. Roanoke sits in a great hollow surrounded by peaks, and we were then in possession of the town and all its buildings, though as a matter of policy the Army of the North Star quartered neither its troops nor its horses on the citizens. There was a church converted to a hospital on the square, but Brown was not kept there; the men knew he was badly wounded, but still, Kagi and especially Tubman wanted no one to see him in his humiliation. I was his orderly and the only one not turned away. It was the Doc and not I who mixed his powders that day. I had been working with Doctor Hunter for two years now (the same who had saved my life three years before), but he looked like an old man now, even though he was not yet thirty. Like Brown (like myself) he had lost his family in the war. He certainly looked like an old man after the work of that day, after he entered the house and came out and nodded to the others. Tubman looked fiercely around at the hills. Kagi wept, one of two times I ever saw him weep, the other being the day we buried Green. Doc looked just tired and worn. I was honored that he came and stood beside me, of everyone there: not as if I were his apprentice but as if I were, even at fifteen, his colleague. He didn't weep and neither did I, for we were medical men. But I weep now, unashamed, an old man, almost fifty years later, not for Brown—God knows the Captain lived to see more of his dreams come true than most of us—I weep with some kind of joy remembering the square silently filling up with soldiers as twilight fell, mostly n'African but some foreign, some Merican, even the silk-bloused Mexican Garibaldini, (many of them black recruits by now) speaking that wild lingo I thought was Italian until I went to Italy. Nobody had to tell the men that Shenandoah Brown was dead. There was a drum roll, the longest I have ever heard. Tubman gave a nod, and the red, black, and green flag that I had first seen on the lawn at Green Gables, with Cricket's arm around my shoulders—that mighty flag dipped three times and swung up high again. A thousand rifles fired into the air in a great rippling wave of sound; one shot each, or Captain Brown would, I think, even then have had their hides. And on the mountains that surrounded Roanoke on every side, a fire sprang to life—two, four, six of them, lighted on the top of each of the brooding peaks that had nurtured our rebellion and birthed our independence.

Then we all went back to war.

☆ ☆ ☆

Harriet loved the singing.

From the rear observation platform of the southbound *John Brown,* she could feel the hum of the plasma motors in her bones rather than her ears, like a hymn. The ship was quiet. A lot of people slept on airships even in the daytime, and soon it would be midnight. Her mother was asleep with her head on her daughter's lap. Harriet was glad the car hadn't gotten fixed: she loved to fly. The car was in the cargo hold, courtesy of the Harper's Ferry Museum. Even old Cardwell didn't seem to mind. "Half of success is failing," he had said. "Now I know what won't work."

Moving carefully so she wouldn't wake her mother, Harriet touched the ivory, folded-over tops of her shoes; they dropped to the floor, where they nestled together so they wouldn't get separated.

The ship was so steady on its microwave beam that it seemed it was the long dark spine of the Blue Ridge that was moving, gliding past, like a cloud or a hundred-mile-long air creature.

It was midnight. It was good to have her mother back. Her father in many ways she felt had never left: every time Harriet looked up at the night sky, she saw him there. But it seemed to satisfy her mother to have watched them place the little plaque on the red stone on the faraway planet he had dreamed of and loved and orbited, but never touched. Mama and Grandmother had of course cried, along with Katie Dee, and sixty people cried with them, some in the front yard. Half of Staunton wanted to share the moment with the Lion's mother; and Harriet, her mother, and Grissom, six hours late, had barely been able to squeeze into the little house. So much for worrying that Pearl would be watching it all alone.

Grissom had brought them in his little hummer, and even stayed for a piece of chess pie. He was an expert at relating to old people.

The world below was as dark as the night at the end of the first day. Lights were scattered up and down the valley, showing mankind's work: still so meager compared to the stars.

12:45. According to the slowly moving line on the liquid-crystal display in the lounge, they had just crossed into Nova Africa. Harriet looked down for a sign of the border, but it was just one dark, sleeping world from up here.

A few night people were in the far corner of the lounge watching vid: LIFE DISCOVERED ON MARS! Her Dad would have liked that. Harriet would have gotten up to watch, but she didn't want to wake her mother. Besides, she was tired too. She was glad to be going home. She had a year of school to look forward to, and though she hadn't yet dared mention it to her mother, her first actual flight training.

Plus a new baby brother, on the way.

Plus such beautiful shoes.